When the
Nightingale Sings

Edited by
JOYCE CAROL THOMAS

A GATHERING OF FLOWERS
Stories about Being Young in America

When the Nightingale Sings

JOYCE CAROL THOMAS

HarperCollins*Publishers*

Library of Congress Cataloging-in-Publication Data
Thomas, Joyce Carol.
  When the nightingale sings / by Joyce Carol Thomas.
    p.   cm.
  Summary: Despite her mean-spirited foster mother's attempts to demean her, fourteen-year-old orphan Marigold finds the song within her heart during the search for a new lead gospel singer for the Rose of Sharon Baptist Church.
  ISBN 0-06-020294-7. — ISBN 0-06-020295-5 (lib. bdg.)
  [1. Singing—Fiction.   2. Self-respect—Fiction.   3. Orphans—Fiction.]
I. Title.
PZ7.T36696Wh   1992   92-6045
[Fic]—dc20   CIP
                                                                  AC

Typography by Christine Kettner
2   3   4   5   6   7   8   9   10
❖

To Mama

*A very special thanks
to my very special editors,
Joanna Cotler and Susan Hill,
and
to my wonderful agent,
Mitch Douglas*

Rise up, my love . . . and come away.
For, lo! the winter is past,
the rain is over and gone;
the flowers appear on the earth
and the time of the singing of birds is come. . . .
                    Song of Solomon 2:10

CONTENTS

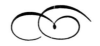

PROLOGUE

IN SOUTH Sweet Earth on a palm-tree point near the Swamp grew delicate orchids, lacy cypress, custard apples, giant mangroves, and an orphan called Marigold.

Unbeknownst to her, many miles away in north Sweet Earth, on the other side of the Swamp, lived her aunt Letty, fondly called Queen Mother Rhythm because she reigned as lead gospel singer in the Rose of Sharon Baptist Church.

This is the story of Marigold, an orphan born in the Swamp. Her birth is a mystery about to unfold. . . .

LULLABY

I

N A STAINED-GLASS church in north Sweet
Earth near the Swamp, the gospel choir was
carrying on something wonderful. You could
feel the splash on your shoulders, they sang
the notes to "Have You Been to the Water"
so convincingly. My lands, they sang the
song so well that if you were a heathen and
hadn't been to the water to be baptized, when
they got through with you, you had been
dipped and almost drownded by the preacher
and hadn't been anywhere near a creek.

Well, in the midst of all this singing and

"Hallelujahing" a Swamp Woman appeared. You could tell she was from deep in the Swamp because she had on the costume of the Swamp people, kind of like a Swamp bird with ruby colors and a plum-dyed scarf tied around her head. And muddy, muddy shoes.

Swamp people never come to church. And they most certainly never attend Rose of Sharon Baptist.

Well, she broke up the service.

The preacher rose up from his chair in the pulpit. Queen Mother Rhythm, the mother of the church, sometimes called Sister Letty, unwrapped her mouth from around that song. And the choir stopped rocking midswing.

"Anybody here named Queen Mother Rhythm?" the Swamp Woman, speaking in a rushed voice, wanted to know.

"Yes," Letty answered. "They call me Queen Mother Rhythm."

"There's a woman trying to give birth down yonder washed up in the Swamp, and she's calling for you."

"For me?" answered Letty. "I don't know anybody laying up around here. And anyway, why would she be calling for me?"

The Swamp woman shrugged, then added in a bitter voice, "Probably got abandoned by some old trifling dream. Looking for a rainbow and got waylaid by lightning. Hoped to plant her feet on higher ground. 'Stead she ended up lower than the Swamp, in the damn quicksand!"

The choir members let out a big "Umph, umph, umph," followed by a "My, my, my" at the sound of the word "damn."

Catching herself, the Swamp Woman, reminded that she was standing in a church house, made the sign of the cross and backed out the sanctuary door, saying to Letty, "Follow me!"

Letty, rushing to keep up with the agitated woman, signaled two of the choir members, Annie Mae and Betty Jean, to follow her.

To Letty's many questions the Swamp Woman fussed, "I don't know. I'm just come to get you. No telling what's bothering her. Woman's trying to bring new life into the world, but if you ask me, I think she's dying. Poor soul. Say she given so much, ain't enough left for her ownself. Say she ask your forgiveness."

"*My* forgiveness?" said Letty.

"Say she given birth to two dead children. Say she want to make sure this one live even if she don't. Was coming, she claimed, to give her newborning child to you, Queen Mother Rhythm. Uh-huh, that's exactly what she said."

"I don't understand it. I don't understand it at all, but we'd best hurry," said Letty, almost skipping through the palm trees to keep up with the quick-legged Swamp Woman.

Annie Mae and Betty Jean, the singers from the Voices of Paradise Choir, hopped over bushes, ducked under mangrove tree limbs, and skirted the hanging moss and little shimmering pools of water that let them know they were deep in the Swamp.

Just as they passed a patch of wildflowers, Letty paused. "I think I hear . . ." she said, leaning her curly head forward. "I think I hear my sister's voice. I do! That is my sister's voice. That's Melissa's voice! I'm coming, Melissa! She's sounding fainter and fainter! Melissssa!"

"Right over here," said the Swamp Woman, pointing.

And Melissa lay on the ground near a mangrove tree, her clothes in rags, with a new baby girl, wrapped in a shredded shawl, cuddled in her arms.

"Letty, is that really you?" she asked through cracked lips in a small, feeble voice. "I hear they call you Queen Mother Rhythm."

"Melissa," said Queen Mother Rhythm. "Yes, this here's Letty."

"Come closer," said Melissa.

Letty stooped down to study her sister's face.

"Don't worry about me, Letty. I know I look awful. I don't believe I'm gonna make it. But would you look at this little piece of heaven in my arms?"

Dumbstruck, Letty stared at the baby. Then she started to ask, "When . . ."

With a wave of her hand Melissa cut Letty off from speaking. "No, please, don't talk. It's too late. You'll see when you read my letters. They're right here with the baby. See inside her shawl?"

"Oh," said Letty, spying the packet tied with speckled green ribbons.

"You'll understand when you read them later. But take her. Letty . . ."

Melissa started to say something else but began coughing and couldn't stop.

Letty took the baby from Melissa, swaddling the shawl with its pack of ribbon-tied letters tighter around the child. She commenced rocking the baby as she talked. "Now, Melissa," said Letty, "I don't hold anything against you. It's not in my heart. Forget about the past."

Melissa's head suddenly drooped on her chest. And Letty let out a pain-filled groan. "Melissa, now, Melissa, wait!"

Letty gave the baby to the Swamp Woman, who was kneeling near a clump of wild marigolds. Terrified, Letty started shaking Melissa.

"Lord! She's gone," Letty cried, even as she tried to rock her sister back to life.

Still stunned, Letty finally raised up off her knees to go take the baby from the Swamp Woman.

But the Swamp Woman was not there,

and neither was the baby.

Letty thrashed around in the bushes behind the mangrove tree, trampling down pickerel weeds and blue-and-white vines, crushing the petals of marigolds and golden orchids, but she couldn't find the baby.

"All right," she said to Annie Mae and Betty Jean, "which one of you all's holding the baby? Hand her over."

"We don't have her," said the choir members. "We haven't moved."

And sure enough, when Letty looked over at the singers, she saw they had not moved from under the two palm trees where she left them when she first ran to Melissa. They were so caught up in the drama of the long-lost sisters, they were rooted to the spot.

"Well where is she?" asked Letty. "Melissa gave me the baby. I handed her to the Swamp Woman. She was right there by those marigolds. She's gone? Search around. Here, you go that way. You, strike out over yonder. Where can she be? Lord?

"I know good and well I handed her to that Swamp Woman. Under this tree by these marigolds. I know it was right here!" echoed

Letty, over and over again, like a stuck record. But none of that helped; the baby was gone. They searched ~~unitl~~ until there was no more light.

When Letty saw the sliver of a moon and knew they had to leave the swamp, the wind seemed to go out of her and stay out. She dragged herself over to the shawl-covered body of her sister Melissa. And stood quiet for a long, long time. Finally she spoke to the ghost of the woman.

"Well, Melissa, you always were the best singer. Voice so sweet. So sorrowful. So songful. I promise you I'm going to find that baby."

Betty Jean whispered to Annie Mae as they stood and waited almost at attention, "What happened? We've got to find that baby!"

And Letty, looking far off, said to no one in particular, "If we ever find her, I'll know her by the Swamp sound in her song."

And Letty sang, "Something kind of precious. Something kind of dear." The warm, cool colors of the Swamp's golden lilies bloomed between the song's verses. And somewhere remembering the colors of marigolds, the baby listened, then turned toward the shadows of notes. At times wispy as Spanish moss, the notes trembled all over her. Then there came a long, long silence. And the child felt a gentle wind leap through the waterweeds and enter her swaddling cloth. And all at once the warm, cool song was inside her, spinning, swimming, and staining the lakes of her heart.

"What I barely remember is this,
a Swamp-stained lullaby."

Marigold

MARIGOLD

ON THE SOUTH EDGE of the forest-thick Swamp in a corner of a ramshackle cottage, fourteen-year-old Marigold bent her braided head over a notebook. She sat near the open window, where she could smell spicewood and hear a washing rain breaking through the willows and sugarcane.

In curls and slants of tree-green ink her right hand shaped these words:

Something kind of precious

"Put that ink pen down," said Cousin Ruby, interrupting Marigold's train of thought.

Her foster mother demanded that Marigold call her Cousin instead of Mama. "And what, may I ask, was that song you was humming while you was writing?"

"I don't know," said Marigold, closing her notebook. "Just some old song."

"I never heard it on the radio before."

"I didn't get it off the radio. Sometimes it just comes."

"Well, Miss, if I hear you singing to any-body but us, I'm gonna cut your tongue out and throw it in the Swamp for the crocodiles to eat."

Just then Arlita, one of the twins sitting over on the couch munching fried potatoes and sipping sun tea, piped up, "She didn't sing us to sleep last night, Mama, like you told her to do."

"I sang until you fell into a deep sleep."

Arlita, frowning, said, "See, Mama, she knows that's not true. I couldn't sleep. But Marigold, you were the one sleeping, so deep you looked like you'd fell into a faint."

"Uh-huh," said Carita. "Like her voice, faint."

Arlita, chewing and speaking at the same time with her mouth crammed full of food, said in a garbled voice, "Well, Marigold, when you do try to sing with some authority, you screech loud enough to call the hogs. By the way, did you slop them pigs yet?"

"I did," said Marigold, putting the top back on her pen.

Then the other twin jumped on her. "What about our dresses?" asked Carita, hungrily chewing on a stump of sugarcane. "Did you finish that green dress for me? We have an audition."

"An audition," said Marigold. "How I wish—"

Cousin Ruby snapped, "Wish all you want, but I'm the one told them to come way down here to this side of the Swamp. They think they got all the talent up there where they are, but I can show them a thing or two. My daughters! Took ten letters before they agreed to come. For *my* daughters. Don't nobody want to listen to your little squeaky voice, Marigold. We just have you sing to us for our amusement. Your voice is only good for to tickle us with. Nothing nightingalelike about it. They're trying to find a new nightingale. That Queen Mother Rhythm is so tired she must be ready to retire! I've finally got her Royal Runners to come out here, and I know the nightingale's gonna be one of you girls."

"A nightingale!" said Marigold wistfully.

Arlita snapped, "Nightingale, not nightmare. Tell her, Mama."

And Cousin Ruby continued berating Marigold: "Marigold, how many times do I have to tell you you can't sing? The best you can do is go out and sell eggs so we can keep poverty 'way from the door. You sound 'bout as bad as you did that day your evil mama brought you by here and abandoned you in the bushes. Oh, you was squawling and bawling, yelping and yapping like some old stray dog. We took you in when your own didn't want you."

Cousin Ruby was all stirred up for some reason. Marigold could never quite figure out Ruby Lee's moods; she always seemed to be having a bad spell. Now her entire face was changing like an overcast sky, going from cloudy to stormy. But the main question that haunted Marigold was why the woman treated her so bad.

Suddenly Cousin Ruby's eyes settled on the fabric piled on top of the old Singer sewing machine. And she picked up a half-finished dress.

"And see here, this is the thanks we get," said Cousin Ruby, craning her neck. "This seam's crooked. This was supposed to be finished yesterday."

Marigold answered in a sinking voice, "But I had four of them to sew. I finished two, and with selling the eggs, wringing the chickens' necks and picking the feathers off them, peeling the potatoes, baking the bread, scrubbing the floors, emptying the trash, and combing all you-all's heads, I haven't had time to even look in the mirror."

"Another thing," interrupted Cousin Ruby, "don't be looking in no mirrors. That's right up there with singing. I don't want to see it. We'll tell you how you look, which is awful. We'll tell you how you sound, which passed awful and met up with pitiful. I don't want to hear it, that sorry voice, unless you're singing to us. A comedy act."

"That's right," chimed Arlita. "Duck your head when you pass a mirror."

Cousin Ruby continued, "Now I want those dresses finished if you have to stay up all night. Queen Mother Rhythm's Minister of Music is coming to audition my daughters, and they have to look nice."

Carita, not wanting to be left out of the fussing, added, "And Mama, she didn't teach us that song you told her to."

"I did so," said Marigold. "You just sang the notes wrong."

Cousin Ruby put her hands on her hips and said, "Well, Miss, you teach it to them till they sing the notes right."

"Nobody taught me how to sing," said Marigold in a soft voice.

Now Cousin Ruby was wagging her fingers all up in Marigold's face; like a full-blown hurricane her voice thundered, "Your case is different. Anybody whose mama leaves her in the bushes is supposed to know how to fend for herself. In other words, is supposed to *sing for her supper.*"

"Thought you said I couldn't sing," said Marigold, so quietly Cousin Ruby had to lean forward.

"What you say?"

"Thought you said I couldn't sing," Marigold repeated a little louder.

"Clucking. That's what that is. A long way from real singing like my sweet little twins are capable of."

Now the twins hunched up together and began one of their little teasing numbers, especially reserved for Marigold.

Carita sang out first, "Somebody put a hurt on her, that's why she clucks so sweet, left her a motherless child."

"That's right," picked up Arlita, dancing around poor Marigold. "Oh how she waited for that mama to come, left her in the bushes."

"Yes, and took off and run," added Carita.

"Oh, she can cluck all right," agreed Cousin Ruby. "That's why we got her selling chicken eggs."

The twins speeded up the ditty, egged on by their mother.

Carita teased, "She screeches and moans all between the notes."

"Sets the roosters to fanning, mesmerizes the goats," chanted Arlita.

Cousin Ruby laughed meanly and added, "You better do all I tell you and some I don't."

The twins kept up the hurtful teasing: "Daddy deserted her in the lurch, he's a father ain't got child the first."

After the twins finished, Cousin Ruby said, in a stiller voice, "You'd better teach my daughters well, Marigold. Get the notes straight. I can't stand all those dogs barking."

Marigold said with some bite in her gentle voice, "That's what dogs do, bark." Then added under her breath, "Especially when they don't like what they be hearing."

Carita, who didn't hear Marigold's aside, said, "All that barking's enough to make a body puffy under the eyes."

Marigold ventured a little louder, "That's because your eyes have seen the glory of the coming of the Lord."

Carita widened her eyes and said, "Mama, did you hear that?"

Marigold had miscalculated. Cousin Ruby had not reached the end of her rage yet, for she picked up the broom and started chasing Marigold around the room. "Don't (*swing*) be (*swing*) talking (*swing*) to my daughters (*swing*) in that lackluster (*swing*) voice. Teach (*swing*) them some music!"

In a grating voice the twins crackled, "Get out of our sight for now." And Marigold fled outside past the neat flower garden and stopped by the pond lined with golden lilies, where she started singing one of the three songs she had made up that morning. She knew the words by heart. In a liquid voice she sang clearly, the lyrics asking, "How can I not sing?"

She had just reached the part that went, "Showers of light, nightingales in flight, lift up their wings, and I can't help but sing," when Anthony, Queen Mother Rhythm's Minister of Music, and his Royal Runners, River Rainbow and Sparrow Sunrise, knelt down to drink from the stream at the other end of the pond.

Anthony's tall and lanky figure came to attention at the sound of Marigold's voice. Intelligent eyes, black as a black sparrow's, tried to see who was singing. Anthony and the Royal Runners downstream and downwind from Marigold rose up but, because of the thicket of loblolly pines and bushes, could hear very clearly every turn of note but could not see the singer.

"What a lovely voice," Anthony exclaimed. "According to our map, it's coming from the direction of the home of the twins. Surely here we'll find that voice. That's our nightingale. Whoever sings those notes must have a soul with shiny wings. At last!"

Anthony, moving gracefully, with a wild-cat stride, his Royal Runners in tow, hurry-walked up to the cottage excited about seeing the person who belonged to the voice they'd just heard. He knocked on the door.

"Come in, come in," said Cousin Ruby, letting the three auditioners enter. "My twin daughters await you. See how they're ready to receive you?"

Anthony surveyed the buck-toothed twins with dismay. He had come such a long distance. He felt so tired, his eyes itched with the irritation of swamp sand, and he rubbed them as if to dispel the unsettling vision of the twins; he had wanted so much to find the new nightingale even if it meant journeying this far from Rose of Sharon. Looking at the twins, he asked himself if he had come all this way down south to the ends of the earth plus five miles, for nothing. Then he remembered that sometimes the best music came from the most unlikely sources.

"See how they're ready to receive you?" repeated Cousin Ruby.

"Well, yes . . ." Anthony said hesitantly.

"Might as well get started," Cousin Ruby said with a beaming smile.

Carita and Arlita, in their best dresses, hair in tight curls, struck their best posture and waited for the signal from their mother.

"Carita, dear, sing full-throated now. Arlita, stick out your chest, sweetheart."

When the twins opened their mouths, Anthony got set to hear repeated the lovely song he'd heard on the way. But the expression on his face quickly turned to agony. Here were no nightingale voices. He wanted to cover his ears and run. Their squawking echoed the croaks of Swamp frogs and crow-'fore-day roosters. He gritted his teeth and finally said in the middle of the chorus, "Please, I think we've heard enough. Is there anyone else in your family who sings?"

Cousin Ruby said, "Nobody else but me. You know, I have a wonderful soprano voice. Why in my younger days I sang just like a nightingale. That's why my daughters are so gifted, you see—they got it from me."

"Perhaps—" began Anthony.

Cousin Ruby kept bragging, trying to make her speaking voice sound like a poet's, "In my other life I was a bird. In my other life I sat on God's shoulder. He heard every word."

"Thank you," said Anthony, adding under his breath, "I was sure I heard another voice."

Hurriedly, Cousin Ruby added, "Nobody here but us and a few chickens."

"Are you certain?" asked Anthony.

The Royal Runners, River Rainbow and Sparrow Sunrise, quickly came to the rescue. "Let's go. I think we done heard enough."

Cousin Ruby was still promoting her

charges. "You'll call for a second audition. Yes, I can see it in your eyes. You loved my daughters."

But Marigold, not knowing that Anthony had heard her voice, and having only just come near the house, peered in the window, and heard Cousin Ruby's last comment.

She whispered to herself, "Oh, please do call for a second audition, or they'll beat me half to death for not working a miracle with those ugly voices."

Anthony, his back to the window, answered Cousin Ruby's statement that he loved her daughters' singing with "I did?"

"We have another appointment," said Sparrow Sunrise impatiently. "We must hurry along, Anthony."

And Anthony's voice in that one phrase, "I did?" suggested sugarcane and custard apples and rainbows and the musky smell of mangrove trees.

For the first time Marigold felt an emotion beyond the puppy love she used to feel for boys sometimes. Beyond the crushes on schoolteachers. This time the feeling had as much to do with her as it had to do with him.

She felt as light as loblolly pines swaying in the wind.

Anthony, relieved to be pulled away from this pitiful audition, but sad he had not discovered whom he had hoped to discover, turned to leave. At that moment Marigold saw his peat-mixed-with-clay brown face and those intelligent, ink-black eyes for the first time.

But all she said out loud was "He's the most handsome thing I've ever seen!"

"What was that?" asked Anthony.

"What?" asked the Royal Runners, the twins, and Cousin Ruby all together.

"Oh, that wasn't anything," said Cousin Ruby, laughing nervously. "We got a lot of chipmunks 'round here in these here woods. Sometimes they make so much noise, they sound just like real people talking. Uh-huh."

Outside the cottage Anthony, with the Royal Runners stepping and singing behind him, walked disappointedly away. While he might be crestfallen, River Rainbow and Sparrow Sunrise were finally able to get out some good belly laughs that they had been holding in all the time they were inside

Cousin Ruby's place. River Rainbow said to Sparrow Sunrise, in rap style, making it up as they trotted along:

> *One's too thick*
> *One's too slight*
> *One's too dull*
> *One's not bright*
> *But worst of all one child can't sing*
> *And the other's voice got a false ring*
> *And the mama, Lord have mercy!*

Sparrow Sunrise, hip-hopping in the same rap style as River Rainbow, added a new verse. He didn't want to be outdone by his friend, so he added moves to every muscle in his body, like a dangling skeleton at Halloween, his toes twinkling and stepping sideways and back and forth, dipping in and out of rhythm. Now and then they'd both clap their hands together and syncopate the beat.

> *The song's out of rhyme*
> *The beat's out of time*
> *Queen Mother Rhythm won't like this*
> *No, she won't*
> *No, she don't*

But worst of all one child can't sing
And the other's voice got a false ring
And the mama, Lord have mercy!

Every time the Royal Runners would rap "And the Mama, Lord have mercy!" they did a little skipping dance.

Anthony walked along, his hands behind his back, still thinking deeply, lost in thought, savoring the way the mystery voice had sounded when he had first heard it by the pond.

"You-all be quiet and quit clowning," he said. "I'm trying to think."

"He's trying to think," the Royal Runners said in unison, burst out laughing, and when shot a glance by Anthony, hushed up.

Marigold, thoroughly enchanted by Anthony, followed along out of sight.

And Anthony said out loud, "Where is the angel whose voice I heard?"

Marigold had been convinced by her foster mother and the foster sisters that her voice was all squawking, and not knowing he'd overheard her sing, she said, "Oh he's lovesick. I wish it was my voice he pined for."

She was so taken by his longing, she started to sing a little song too: "If I was the one, I'd run to his side, I'd run, if I was the one."

"Did you hear something?" asked Anthony.

"What?"

"A note," he said, stopping. "Like a whisper of a song."

But Marigold was so busy singing, she didn't hear Anthony's response.

"I didn't hear anything," said Sparrow Sunrise.

River Rainbow said, "Did kind of sound like that girl we heard on the way."

After she stopped singing, Marigold asked herself, "What would he want with a girl like me, when he has an angel on his mind? A girl like me who gets mistreated so much. Must be something wrong with me. My own mama didn't want me. And why does Cousin Ruby treat me so mean? What would he want with a girl like me?" At that point Marigold turned around and started back to the cottage.

"Marigold! Marigold!" Cousin Ruby

yelled. "Where the heck did that gal git to? Oh there you are, hiding someplace, probably trying to sing one of them songs you be trying to make up. You'd better get to hawking them eggs before they hatch, you lazy heifer!"

And Marigold put on her little ruffled apron that she always wore when selling eggs and started out.

All the time she was walking up and down the road with her basket of eggs, calling, "Eggs? Eggs? Fresh Eggs," she was thinking about Anthony.

"Girlie," said a gray-haired granny, "these eggs ain't so old they 'bout rotten, is they?"

"No, ma'am," said Marigold. "Hens just got up off them. See here, feel, they're still warm from their feathers."

"All right, then, I'll take a dozen."

She moved around in a kind of daze, a little put out with herself that she couldn't get *him* off her mind. After all, he did love somebody else, and here she was pining after a fellow whose heart was already taken.

But the feeling wouldn't go away. She kept seeing those intelligent eyes, the color of a black sparrow's, of ebony wisdom, and his peat-and-clay brown skin. When the last egg had been sold from her basket, she turned around on the road and started back to the cottage.

In that house it was hard for her to keep her courage up. She usually found refuge in writing, and so she sat at her place in the corner trying to write. But today the snide remarks from the twins fell on sensitive ears.

The twins sat on the floor with books trying to do their homework and meddle Marigold at the same time.

"Just look at her," said Arlita. "She got hips like a horse."

"Lips like a lizard," crowed Carita.

"They call her Marigold, but she ain't no flower. She just a weed!"

Now the teasing reached a point where Marigold couldn't take any more. "I don't feel so good," Marigold said aloud.

"That's just an excuse. How dare you get sick when we need your help?"

"You know summer school's not the easiest way to make up our grades."

Marigold started to stand up but felt dizzy and sat back down.

The twins soon realized they couldn't continue teasing Marigold if she was acting sick, so they struck out at each other.

"Now look what you gone and done," Arlita spat at Carita. "How'm I gonna get my math done?"

"You're the one made her sick," charged Arlita. "And I've got an essay due in my summer English class! And I still haven't figured out the difference between a verb and a noun. If Marigold won't help me, I'm lost! She's turned death ears to us!"

"Deaf ears, not death ears," Marigold said wearily. She looked at the notebook on the table.

Suddenly she wanted to continue writing down the song that had been haunting her. It was a musical memory. The idea of it swept strength all over her, from her head to her toes. The twins, caught up now in fussing and blaming each other, paid no attention to her. "My heart insists," she whispered to herself as she picked up her pen and began to add green lyrics to the line she had started earlier:

Something kind of precious
Something kind of dear

Just as she finished writing the word "dear" and was thinking on adding to the lyrics, she heard the door slam and knew that Cousin Ruby was home. No telling when she'd get to finish the song.

"Why aren't you two doing your homework?" Cousin Ruby asked Carita and Arlita, who were sitting in the middle of the floor with their lips stuck out.

"She won't help us," they moaned.

"Marigold!" said Cousin Ruby. "Git your mean self out of that notebook and git to helping these girls with their homework. I don't want to tell you but once."

"All right," said Marigold. "Y'all come on," she said, closing her notebook and making space at the table for the twins.

THE MYSTERIOUS
SWEET JIMMY

O N THE NORTH SIDE of the Swamp, inside Rose of Sharon Baptist Church, choir rehearsal with the Voices of Paradise shifted
into full swing. Betty Jean said, "Can't we
take a break now? We've been here over an
hour and haven't hardly paused between
hymns and gospel numbers."

Queen Mother Rhythm, the lead voice in
the choir, was the first to sit down in the
pew and pick up the mortuary fan and start
fanning herself.

"Speaking of taking a break," she said, "I

repeat: It's about time I took one from the choir forever. It's been a long journey. And time is moving on. This here is life. You don't get out of here alive."

"Oh, you're not ready to leave the choir yet," said Annie Mae in a pleading voice.

"Yes, I believe I just might be."

"Ain't nobody can take your place," said Betty Jean.

"It's not *my* place. This place belongs to the nightingale. And once she decides to come, nothing can stop her," said Queen Mother Rhythm. "I believe there's someone somewhere. Somebody with an angel voice. Yesterday 'round about dusk, thought I heard it. Song had a soul with flowers in between the notes. Now if we could just find that singer . . ."

Annie Mae piped up, "The Royal Runners have been looking steady, just like you asked them to. Auditioning here and there. They sent another group in from Little Willow."

Betty Jean said, "Little Willow? Don't bother. I already heard them practicing. Uh-huh, sounding like they just broke free from getting their necks wrung. It's a whole bunch of water turkeys sitting up in there. Where's the nightingale in the bunch?"

Annie Mae said, "The only way to tell is to listen to a lot of different singers. That's the only way to find somebody to take your place, Queen Mother Rhythm."

Betty Jean added, "The Royal Runners've been to the south. They've been to the north. The west. And the east. Let them tell it, they've seen every bird that opened her mouth to shape a note. And haven't found her yet."

"Maybe the nightingale's gone extinct," said Annie Mae.

"Last night I dreamed," Queen Mother Rhythm began.

"Dreamed?" asked Annie Mae. "Dreamed what?"

"That I heard the most beautiful sound . . ." continued Queen Mother Rhythm.

Betty Jean leaned over to Annie Mae and whispered, "Maybe it was one of those Hurricane Women hollering. My granddaddy seen one once. Walking through the Swamp. She had long windy legs and arms that could wrap around ten trees. He smiled at her crooked, my granddaddy said, and he's still suffering. Said that Hurricane Woman raised one long leg and gave him rheumatism of the mind!"

"Shut up about them. Hurricane Women. Humph. It was a holy sound," said Queen Mother Rhythm.

Betty Jean said aside, "You ever wanted something so bad you imagine it? She ain't heard nothing but them barnyard birds squawking 'fore day."

Queen Mother Rhythm said, "I know what I heard, and it wasn't a laying hen no-how. Sun hadn't risen. Full moon was on my face."

"Well how come none of the rest of us heard it?" said Betty Jean.

Queen Mother Rhythm figured, "Probably snoring so loud you couldn't hear your own self breathe, let alone heavenly music!"

"Guess she told you," said Annie Mae.

This time Betty Jean spoke a little softer and held a hand up to her mouth. "She's hearing ghosts. Haints."

But Annie Mae answered compassion-ately, if just as quietly, "The specter of a singer silenced. The memory of her one sister gone from her without any hope of reconcilia-tion. Then on top of that lost her other dead sister's daughter before she even got her good. The story of three sisters. That's the memory worrying her. Is it any wonder that she, poor thing, hears what ain't even there?"

"Her nerves. It's her nerves. Her feathers get a little rough," crackled Betty Jean.

But Queen Mother Rhythm was too busy talking to hear the two women gossiping. She was explaining her decision to the choir. "I've been ministering to the sick, singing to the downhearted, hollering 'cross cane fields and swamps, and good Lord, I'm tired!"

"Deacon Brown got wrecked in a wreck and Little Joe Wonder got hurt in a hurri-cane. They both called for Queen Mother Rhythm," said Betty Jean.

"Uh-huh."

All between Queen Mother Rhythm's speech to the choir, Betty Jean, with her sense of humor, was having fun. She whis-pered to Annie Mae, "And then the drought 'bout dried us out. Greens tasting like grits. We sure needed Queen Mother Rhythm's miracle music then!"

In spite of herself, Annie Mae giggled and Queen Mother Rhythm shot her a glance.

Betty Jean continued, "Sometimes I think these Royal Runners don't know gold from brass. Dumb as two shovels."

Queen Mother Rhythm said, "Good thing I sent Anthony, our Minister of Music, with his Royal Runners. If anybody can find a voice, that Anthony can. My patience has about run clean out. I'm telling you, choir, I'm ready to fold up."

Feeling guilty about laughing, Annie Mae spoke up in a sober tone, "Please, Queen Mother Rhythm, don't do that. Wait a little bit more. We'll find her."

"All right, folks, the break is over." And Queen Mother Rhythm started another song, with a short solo lead.

Real low, Annie Mae said to Betty Jean, "I hear that yearning in Queen Mother Rhythm's moaning and singing. Everybody's in pain. Of course Queen Mother Rhythm can't travel like she used to, from place to place. People who want to hear her have to come within the sound of her voice. And she won't sing long. Just gives us a little taste of the magic."

Betty Jean said, sucking her bottom lip, "Humph. Just hope her voice don't leave on away from here before we find another one to replace it."

"Mean, mean, mean!" said Annie Mae.

Betty Jean fussed, "The shut-ins out in east Sweet Earth threatening heart attacks and having strokes all because she's too tired to move around and sing."

Annie Mae allowed, "We're trying to hold it together, and those old Royal Runners are stepping 'round like roosters. You think they're really looking in all those places they visit?"

Betty Jean shot back, "For women?" Her voice rising, she said, "Looking's probably most of what they doing. Can't listen for looking."

"Well," said Annie Mae, "I don't know why Queen Mother Rhythm's acting like she's all washed up. Why Reverend Honeywell's been in love with the woman for years.

But she won't pay him no mind. Sweet Jimmy sure did a lot of damage. But every man ain't awful."

"Honey," said Betty Jean, "Sweet Jimmy made an impression. That skunk left a fume Queen Mother Rhythm can't ever wash off."

"'Sweet Jimmy'! Don't say that name too loud around here. It's forbidden."

"You're the one brought it up."

"Now look," said Annie Mae, avoiding the name and the story behind it. "Say for instance she did hook up with Reverend Honeywell. Who's gonna sing strong enough to hold the bond together? Huh? Tell me that?" Then she said after a pause, answering her own question, "If we found that new nightingale, maybe she'd sing at Queen Mother Rhythm and Reverend Honeywell's wedding."

"Wedding?" said Betty Jean. "How do you know he's *that* interested? It's been years! You'd think his desire'd be dead by now."

"When you're in love," Annie Mae declared, "it makes you want to keep on trying. Still, how's she gonna trust any man after what Sweet Jimmy did? I remember what happened just like it was yesterday."

"Uh-huh. Let's talk about it later after choir practice. She's looking our way, and judging from her expression, if I open my mouth one more time she's gonna throw me out of the choir and this choir pew!" said Betty Jean, who managed to give an innocent smile and right on cue sing the first note of the chorus.

WHEN THE
NIGHTINGALE
SINGS

I NSIDE THEIR COTTAGE the twins sat around idle, painting their toenails flaming red as Cousin Ruby berated Marigold about reading instead of working.

"Shakespeare!" she said, picking up a volume of *A Midsummer Night's Dream*. "You don't need to be reading when there's dirt thick as a garden on the windowsill."

Cousin Ruby ran her fingers along the dusty ledge. "I declare I can see squash and turnip greens rooting right before my eyes."

Arlita, looking up from her bad feet, toes sitting on top of toes all due to her vain habit of squeezing her feet into too-small shoes, said, "And she didn't get up all that popcorn spilled from last night. First thing you know, chickens'll be inside the house feeding."

Marigold said under her breath, "They're already here."

"I heard that," said Carita. "Mama, she's acting smart again."

"It's those books," said Cousin Ruby. "Shakespeare, Zora Neale Hurston. That Wolf woman."

"Virginia Woolf," added Marigold, who picked up more books and called out more authors' names: "Phillis Wheatley, Jean Toomer."

Cousin Ruby reached over and knocked the books on the floor. "You're only supposed to read to help the girls with their homework."

Marigold lifted the bucket of vinegar and water and began washing the windows, but Cousin Ruby kept on with her mean words.

"When you get through with the windows and getting into the corners of the floors, Marigold, we got to go. They need some squawking at that outdoors country wedding. No fancy dresses. Marigold, I guess you can do that all right. Didn't I say hurry up? Don't want to be late after all."

"Who's getting married?" asked Carita.

"Wedding's for some of them folks Marigold sell eggs to down at the other end of the road. They must speculate nothing like looking at a bird-legged woman sing to make the groom appreciate the beauty of the bride. Anyway, they promised us a slew of ham hocks. You ain't through yet, Marigold? Hurry up. I can hear them gathering out in the woods."

As angry as she was at Cousin Ruby, Marigold really did look forward to singing. But she didn't want to let Cousin Ruby know this, else she'd figure out some way to take all the joy out of the experience.

And so they walked down the road to the edge of the pond where the wedding party gathered.

The mother of the bride was saying to the gathering of friends and neighbors and relatives, "Can't be rightly joined together if that little orphan girl ain't sung her blessing over the wedding."

The father of the bride nodded in agreement, adding, "Last time two young folks jumped the broom without her voice falling on them like raining rice, the couple split up before the preacher could say, 'Kiss the bride.'"

Before long Marigold's heavenly voice was floating out over the woods as she sang the wedding song "Two." She had made this one up also; she wanted to sing more than the traditional "Here Comes the Bride" just to give herself some variety. She alternated "Two" with "Here Comes the Bride" every other wedding.

> *Together you will stay*
> *To seal this wedding day*
> *Two people must allow*
> *For love to stay somehow*
> *Two people making plans*
> *Two rings upon two hands*
> *To you God bless*
> *To you time's happiness*

It was a simple song, but just lovely enough to make the eyes of the women at the wedding fill with dew.

On the very last note, Cousin Ruby grabbed the bag of ham hocks and rushed Marigold away before people could compliment her good.

"Wish we could stay and celebrate longer," said Cousin Ruby, trying to sound sorry, "but we got to go visit the sick."

"Oh," said the mother of the bride, with much sympathy, "you mean poor sister Willie Mae? She's sinking."

As soon as they got out of hearing distance, on their walk through the sugarcane to Willie Mae's house, Cousin Ruby said, "Marigold, you about the most no-singing child I ever done seen. Sick folks need to hear you screeching just so they can get prepared for that banshee called Death. Here, carry these ham hocks. Bag's so heavy it makes my arms ache."

Because she knew Cousin Ruby so well, Marigold pretended to pout. "Thought I was just gonna sing at a wedding. You didn't say anything about a sick visit."

"I just forgot, that's all. Besides, her husband's gonna pay by giving us some more chickens. Now won't that be nice?" said Cousin Ruby. "Anyway, you don't need to know everything, Miss Smarty. And after the sick, you got to go sing at the baptism. It's at the river right behind Willie Mae's house. The preacher said it might could help if you come sing at the baptism. Being around water might purify your old evil voice. Might sweeten your smart-alecky ways. Though I doubt it."

And Marigold wanted to skip and run— she couldn't think of any place she'd rather be singing than at a baptism! But she held herself back and they walked on to Sister Willie Mae's house, where from a distance they could see her husband, Robert Franklin, hands behind his back pacing back and forth from the house to the porch, going back and forth from Willie Mae's bed to the outside steps.

As they drew nearer Marigold heard him saying to his sick wife, "You can't leave me now, Willie Mae. I just can't let you go!"

Marigold could barely hear the wife's response, for she spoke in a feeble whisper.

"Nothing you can do about it, Robert Franklin."

"There must be something," he said, pacing again.

"You done called the doctors, the nurses, and the missionaries. Nothing else, Robert Franklin, left to do, 'cept maybe call that little orphan girl, Marigold, to help me pass over the River Jordan."

"We didn't call the preacher," said her husband.

"I'm telling you," said Willie Mae, "all I need is that sweet young Marigold."

This sent the husband to the door on his mission when Marigold and Cousin Ruby appeared.

"Good evening, Brother Franklin," said Marigold.

"I was just getting ready . . ." said the husband.

Without any further ados, Marigold went over and spoke to Willie Mae, whose eyes were shining too brightly. Then she reached down and touched the ailing woman, closed her eyes, and sang her song.

I see that angel floating 'round your bed
She says don't be afraid of the path that lies
  ahead
She just wants to welcome you
Hear that clapping of wings

There was a special honey in Marigold's voice when she went into the second verse.

Then Marigold's voice itself seemed to be the wings as she stretched out into the chorus of the song.

Marigold heard a sigh float up from Willie Mae's bed. The sigh kept rising and never came back down but went on through the roof, and since the old woman's eyes were already closed, Marigold did not linger. As she and Cousin Ruby exited, she heard the husband say as he leaned over his wife's bed, "She's gone from the earth, my warmth, my fire, Willie Mae, who brought me water when I was thirsty. Now she's gone, took to the sky. Oh, my wife. All my life."

And because he could not think of anything else to do but pray, he did; before he got up off his knees, he thanked God for the years he'd shared with Willie Mae, promising that every time he pictured his wife, "I will think then of the clapping of wings." Way after a while, he said, "Willie Mae?" Then he looked around him. "Where's that orphan?" he asked the air. "I wanted to thank her."

Marigold and Cousin Ruby had walked around beside the house where they could see candles shining between the trees while the congregation marched to the river two by two singing a song about music. What Marigold liked about baptism in the Swamp was that it was pure drama, it was holy dance, it was tambourines, it was happy clapping. She thought baptism was the most pleasing, the most eye-teasing event she could imagine. And on top of that, the people just wouldn't stay still, even when submerged!

As they neared the river, Marigold stepped from behind a palm tree singing "Have You Been to the Water?" and the people started clapping.

The entire congregation got to rocking by the time she hit that second line, "Have you been baptized?"

They moved as though they had fire all in their feet.

And what Marigold commanded through the song they did.

> *Tonight forget your troubles*
> *Tonight forget your struggles*
> *I know you have had your pain*
> *Salvation is yours to gain*
> *Come on, get in the water*

The preacher was saying, "I baptize you in the name of the Father, the Son, and the Holy Ghost."

And somebody all dressed up in a many-colored cotton sheet would go down, down into the water. They'd come up crying and shouting something joyful. They came through dancing.

"Where's the usherettes?" asked the preacher.

The deacon who was helping him said, "Reverend, even the usherettes supposed to be catching the overcome folks done fell on out themselves!"

> *Have you been to the water?*
> *Have you been baptized?*

"Who'll catch the catchers falling out?"

said the preacher in wonder as he reached for the next candidate for baptism.

"Not me," said the deacon. "That child's song's got me so happy, I got to shout myself!" And the deacon shouted on out of the water, twirled around on a log, turned a flip, and danced through an alley of palms, past the loblolly pines and through the sugarcane, dancing with oblivion, dancing in the spirit.

As the last candidate for baptism came out of the water, Marigold ended the song, which had gone through many key changes, singing:

> Have you been to the water?
> Have you been baptized?
> Hallelujah!

"Sister Marigold's got a gift that just frees the dance in us all," said the preacher.

When Marigold turned to leave, out of the corner of her eye she spied Cousin Ruby taking money from the preacher and hiding it in the folds of her skirt. And in a lightning flash Marigold knew that if Cousin Ruby could, she would take her very voice and give it to the twins.

How in the world did I end up with her? Marigold wondered as they walked home through the golden lilies toward the cottage.

THE TRUTH
ABOUT THE THREE
SISTERS GONE
ASTRAY

MILES AWAY, after choir practice in
Rose of Sharon Baptist Church was over, two
ruby-throated hummingbirds chased and
pestered a red-tailed hawk as she climbed her
mansion of the sky. Beneath them Annie Mae
and Betty Jean, standing on the church steps,
continued to gossip about Queen Mother
Rhythm and a possible marriage between her
and Reverend Honeywell.

"I'd have to vote against it happening,"
said Betty Jean. "Anyway, as I said earlier,
you'd think his desire'd be dead by now."

"Well, love is oxygen. Revives you. Reverend Honeywell's revived. Love make you breathe freer."

"Unless you fall in love, that is, with somebody like—" she hesitated, then looked around to see if anybody was listening before she said the name—"Sweet Jimmy! If true love is oxygen, untrue love must be poison air. Sweet Jimmy! That man! Humph. I remember what happened like it was yesterday. We were just little girls then."

The two Voices of Paradise started reminiscing on that telltale Sunday afternoon when they had been younger, had been part of the audience, and had not yet become members of the Voices of Paradise. On that long ago afternoon Sweet Jimmy had been the MC at a gospel sing-off. And another promoter and Sweet Jimmy were taking "I bound yous" (they didn't use the word "bet" for religious reasons) much the way Annie Mae and Betty Jean were doing. Except instead of wondering about a possible wedding, they were betting on the best singers.

"So far," said Sweet Jimmy, "it's been quite a musical battle. Good voices. But it sounds like my Nightingale Sisters will be the stars of the evening. A hard act to follow."

The promoter said, "Yes, but don't play Regina Redfield and Her Daughters cheap. My girls've been giving the folks fits from Swamp Bird Island to Mangrove Point."

Young Betty Jean had said, "Yon he is: Sweet Jimmy! Child came here charming women in the cradle."

"How'd he get that nickname?" Annie Mae had asked.

"Who?" said Betty Jean, pretending she didn't know who Annie Mae was talking about.

"Sweet Jimmy."

"They say," said Betty Jean, "the man's so sweet, the women don't need cakes and cookies."

"Hmmm," said Annie Mae, who had a schoolgirl crush on the man anyway. "Will his Nightingales put on a show tonight? I wonder."

"You think it's a show up in the choir stand. The best show goes on behind the curtain."

"What you mean?" asked Annie Mae innocently.

"Sweet Jimmy," said Betty Jean, echoing something she'd heard an older usher say, "the man got him three women and they're all sisters."

"What you say?" said Annie Mae, open-mouthed.

Before Annie Mae could clamp her mouth shut, Sweet Jimmy had stepped up to the microphone. And was saying, "And now for your consideration, we're bringing to you our own Nightingale Sisters. Sister Ruby, Sister Melissa, and Sister Letty! Of course you know Sister Letty and Sister Melissa both are among the ten final nominees for Queen Mother Rhythm. So don't forget to vote next month. Put your hands together for our very own Nightingale Sisters!"

The three Nightingale Sisters, dressed in hand-stitched robes, entered and stood at the front center of the choir stand. They sang that song that Melissa had made up and was so famous for, titled "There's a Man in My Life."

Letty started the song off first, singing:

There's a man in my life
He's my king
He's my comforter
He's my friend in deed
He's everything I need
There's a man in my life, Lord

Then Ruby Lee and Melissa sang the chorus in sweet harmony

His name is Jesus
King Jesus
The man in my life

Now Ruby Lee, not as competent a singer as her two sisters, took the lead.

She tried very hard, straining so hard it was almost pitiful.

There's a man in my life
He's there when I need him most
Now I don't like to boast
He's my friend in deed
He's everything I need
There's a man in my life

Then Letty and Melissa sang the chorus in strong harmony. Gentle, guileless.

But when Melissa took the lead, she sang almost seductively. You had to have sharp ears to hear the hint of just a little too much sweetness, and as she was singing she was also looking over at Sweet Jimmy.

There's a man in my life
He's the sweetest savior I know
Good Lord I love him so
He's my friend in deed
He's everything I need
There's a man in my life

After all three had sung the final chorus, the audience applauded as the singers exited behind the curtain. About a minute later a loud commotion could be heard breaking out behind the curtain, upstaging Regina Redfield and Her Daughters, who were standing at the microphone with their mouths open.

In the back, the three sisters continued raising Cain. Ruby Lee said, "Aha! Just as I thought. Get your hands off my husband. I saw you back yonder making eyes at each other. My own sister!"

"Just a little friendly kiss," said Melissa.

"A little too friendly," said Ruby Lee.

"First friends, then lovers."

"Guess you'll find out sooner or later," said Melissa. "My dear sister, I'm not the only one been tasting Sweet Jimmy's honey lips!"

"What do you mean?" asked Ruby Lee as she propped her hands on her hips.

"Ask your big sister," said Melissa.

"Letty?" said Ruby Lee, turning to look at the oldest sister.

"Okay," said Sweet Jimmy, as quiet as the quiet just before a storm. "Y'all settle down. There's an audience out there."

"Audience, my foot!" shouted Ruby Lee. "I don't give a pig's pickle about any old audience. What in tarnation's going on 'round here?"

"He's in love with me," said Melissa.

"I'm the one he wants," said Letty.

"I been meaning to tell y'all," rumbled Sweet Jimmy. "I'm breaking up the group. I finally got some contracts lined up for Melissa. I'm gonna make her a star."

Ruby Lee said, "A star! What about me, your wife?"

Sweet Jimmy said rather patiently,

"Honey, you can't sing. Least not as good as Melissa. And with those two twin babies, one under each arm weighing you down, traveling with you won't be easy. Besides, we already discussed it. Melissa and I'll send money back to you and the kids, once we're established."

"How could you?" said Letty, her voice trembling. "You said you loved me."

Ruby Lee couldn't believe her ears. "You?"

Sweet Jimmy said, "You're all right, Letty, but you see, Melissa's the youngest. And frankly, I got better things in mind. It's easier with one, especially when she's young."

Letty kept shaking her head and tapping her foot. "How can you break up our trio like this? We promised Mama before she died . . ."

In a voice thundering with authority, Sweet Jimmy said, "Let the dead stay dead. This is life. Your mama had visions of back-woods, country revivals on the chitlin circuit where they pay you in fatback and collard greens. A low-class Swamp tour. I'm thinking about higher ground. I'm thinking about Melissa headlining the swankiest swanks.

The only greens I got on my mind is green-backs, not collard greens. Melissa's the one!"

"And I love him," Melissa answered matter-of-factly in a soft, breezy voice.

"True," said Letty, studying her sister, "but do he love you? You been anointed to sing, Melissa. You're gonna drag your gift all up in them Sodom and Gomorrah places where all that drinking and devil's music's going on?"

Ruby Lee, angriest at Melissa, and so stunned she had been silent for almost a whole minute, said, "What y'all gonna do when she has babies?"

"We'll cross that bridge when we get to it," said Sweet Jimmy.

"May you never get to it," said Letty.

"And Letty," said Ruby Lee, "may you never hear a baby cry."

Melissa said, "Watch your mouth, Ruby Lee. You got the least talent. After all, we just tolerated you for Mama's sake." Then she mimicked their mother: "Y'all three stay together."

Ruby Lee said, "Maybe I don't have the

best voice. But nevertheless, my twin daughters will sing."

To which Letty responded, "You might have twins, but I bound you this, they won't sing. We let your husband, who can't sing, take over managing our business. Looks like our business wasn't all he was managing. He can't sing and you can't sing, so how're your daughters gonna sing?"

Ruby Lee, angered by the logic of Letty's statement, shot back with "And you won't have daughter one, good as you can sing!"

"All right, Sweet Jimmy, you choose," said Letty. "Which one will it be?"

"I told you," said Sweet Jimmy quick as lightning. "I already chose. It's a business decision."

Then he took Melissa's hand and went over to a corner of the stage and picked up two suitcases.

At that telling moment, all three sisters almost leaped out of their skins and shouted each to the other two: "Sister, I don't want to see either one of you ever again!"

They all three went their separate ways. And what Annie Mae and Betty Jean remembered was the melody to "There's a Man in My Life" and how the song took on a different meaning when they remembered that while Jesus was the man the song was talking about, somehow the face of Sweet Jimmy also appeared whenever they heard those particular lyrics.

"You know something?" said Betty Jean. "Sweet Jimmy did a lot of damage. But he's the one gave Sister Letty that distinctive sad-joy sound in her voice, and if it wasn't for that triple-timing Sweet Jimmy, she never would've earned the title Queen Mother Rhythm!"

"Now that's the truth," echoed Annie Mae.

CEREMONIES OF THE WIND

∽

THE WIND in the Swamp on the southern end of Sweet Earth was just a little breeze at first, like a mother's kiss on Marigold's cheek. It teased at her dress and rearranged her thick black braids.

And Marigold daydreamed with her pad and pencil. In the arms of a mangrove tree she cradled herself as the light lacing through the cypress tree contemplated her and played with the patterns it let fall over her braids, her eyes, her mouth, her hands.

And Marigold wrote. She went over the verse she had written that first time at home at the table in the corner of the cottage. She was satisfied with the lines. They had been written in a rush, but looking back at them she decided they were fine:

> *Something kind of precious*
> *Something kind of dear*
> *Sparrows light on my fence every morning*
> *Swallows watch me play at noon*
> *Nightingales perch by my bedroom*
> *window*

Her imagination took wings and she finished the first verse and the second verse found her.

She read the two completed verses together and they seemed to fit. She hummed as she went on to the third verse.

She still had not been able to get Anthony out of her mind. As she looked at her new song, she decided it was a good thing she hadn't. She especially liked the line "Something kind of dear."

And the breeze seemed to sing as it played through the leaves of the trees and rustled the leaves in her notebook.

When she pulled her head up from the

pages, she saw the telltale signs: The birds had gone silent. The wind whipped at the leaves, driving eddies of dirt. And the light had gone funny. The air hung heavy with moisture and she was in the midst of danger. Soon a hurricane would be storming through there.

"Oh, good Lord!" she whispered. "Mother in heaven!"

Soowoosh, soo-woosh, soowoosh-woosh-woosh

She got up quickly, clutching her note-book to her breast, and started immediately for home. She would have to take a shortcut, given the way the wind rumbled and rumbled.

Soowoosh, soowoosh, soowoosh-woosh-woosh

But a shortcut could be dangerous. Alligators and crocodiles roamed that part of the Swamp, along with water moccasins and other life-threatening menaces.

"I was so busy writing, I forgot to pay attention," she moaned, chastising herself as she made her way through thick brush deep in the Swamp. She started to skip over a log when mid skip she stopped and fell.

"Good gracious alive! That's no log, that's

a crocodile," she yelled. In the back of her throat she tasted brackish water and fear.

The crocodile showed his huge teeth and flapped his big tail as he waddled in a speedy bowlegged line at her.

For a moment the sight of him paralyzed her. The bumpy, green tough skin. The webbed feet. The awesome teeth. The pop eyes. The cruel intent of his greedy jaws! Then something told her, "Move!"

All atremble she jumped out of the mud and out of the reach of the crocodile's gaping mouth.

Mud streaked her dress. And she couldn't stop shaking.

"My notebook's a mess," she cried as she clutched it tightly with mud-smeared hands.

All the time the wind was picking up speed.

Soowoosh, soowoosh, soowoosh-woosh-woosh

And Marigold speeded up.

She moved almost mindlessly ahead.

Soowoosh, soowoosh, soowoosh-woosh-woosh

This time she stayed clear of the logs, but there were other dangers.

Her foot stepped toward what she thought was firm ground; but the ground did not hold—it pulled her down.

"Quicksand!" she gasped, and all the time she was sinking she was thinking about people who'd gone into the Swamp and never returned. Everybody knew the quicksand had taken them. A burial ground without any kind of digging or funeral rites. The earth welcomed all visitors but never let them loose. In fact the more they struggled, the tighter the earth's hold. All of this was running through Marigold's mind with the speed of light as she was being pulled under.

The Swamp light changed by the hurricane troubled her mind until it was difficult to think. Her heavy feet dragged, lost in the quicksand. And she felt water pushing upward through the swelling sand. She panicked.

The watery grains tugged at her knees and she flailed and kicked and hollered. A bird sang short and calm as the meditating voice of God. She reached for the sound. And missed.

She reached again for the sound and the

earth reached for her hips. She was sinking fast. "Oh my God!" she hollered.

She hollered so long until the very breath left her lungs. A Swamp light lit on her, and when she breathed in, she breathed in the bird's sound and the calmness that lay lined in it.

And with the calmness came memory.

"Turn over on your back and stretch out your arms away from your body. Straight out like wings. And float. Calmly float. Floooat. Caaalmly."

And she was rolling, floating, rolling, floating off the quicksand and onto the firm earth.

She stood up, her legs shaking, her entire body shaking, wet, tired.

The wind flailed around her.

"Good God Almighty," she moaned.

Then she realized that she had lost her notebook. But more than that she had lost the song too. She had lost the song.

And as the hurricane grew, so did her sadness.

She struck out for home, on the lookout

now for crocodiles and pools of quicksand. Upset because all her songs were at the bottom of the quicksand and she'd never get them back. Undone by the hurricane, which grew so fiercely now that it knocked her down.

Between the wild lightning that lit the Swamp trees like lamps and the rebellious thunder that pealed from mangrove to mangrove, the storm mocked the silence. The stinging rain pelted Marigold's face, wet her braids, and twisted them into dripping ropes.

Palm trees toppled around her, custard apples flew through the air, and it seemed that the hurricane aimed itself directly at her, its wind and wet fury popping her down across the back like a whip.

And she was running, feet tattooing fear into the ground, rage mixing with the blood rushing through her body as the wind whistled and the rain drove her with wet lashes.

It was when the hurricane whipped the shoes right off her feet that she stopped.

"I'm sick of you!" Marigold screamed at the hurricane. "Who do you think you are?"

The little dress Marigold had on was thin

as tissue paper. So the hurricane whipped through the space between her dress and slip and tore her dress to shreds.

And Marigold screamed, "Get on away from here! Coming in here eating up my songs! Coming in here knocking down my trees. These trees weren't bothering anybody! And making me almost dinner for the crocodiles and supper for the quicksand!"

Marigold raged on.

The hurricane roared louder, whirling, boiling.

Soowoosh, soowoosh, soowoosh-woosh-woosh

"I'm tired of your mess!" said Marigold. "You ain't nothing but a lightning mama! Knocking people down and you're always hollering!"

Then the hurricane twisted her hair until the roots hurt, until Marigold thought she'd end up bald-headed.

Finally Marigold saw that the hurricane was going to wear her out.

By now she had lost all sense of direction, so she started running in circles, in her white cotton slip, just a-screaming.

And she did not see the silvery box caked with dirt that the hurricane had uprooted; in the midst of all the utter confusion the hurricane had wrought, there was a pulsating quietness about the box, a mysterious waiting. A faint afterglow hovered over it. A pitter-patter of light, driven by low crosswinds, raced around it. And it had its own sky.

SWAMP LIGHT

JUST BEFORE THE STORM hit, when Marigold was seating herself in the elbow of the mangrove tree, Queen Mother Rhythm, Anthony, and the two Royal Runners, were trudging through the Swamp less than a mile from where Marigold sat writing in her notebook, making up her song and singing the melody to herself.

Queen Mother Rhythm said to Anthony, "Now tell me again, young man, you say you heard her? Say you heard our nightingale?"

Anthony nodded, then patiently explained again. "We'd been on the road for nine days, heading south stomping through little islands, byways, and backwoods. We crossed the Snake Trail. It was about ten in the morning. We were on our way to see the twins whose mama'd been bragging about them for so long."

"Yes," remembered Queen Mother Rhythm. "She had written all those letters. And you say they couldn't sing a lick!"

Anthony continued, "You're getting ahead of what happened, Queen Mother Rhythm. We'd stopped for water and then we heard her."

"Oh, Anthony," she said, "I just hope you're right. Tell me again how she sounded."

"Like a rainbow after the storm or a new sunrise," said Anthony.

"Wonder where she lives."

"I don't know," said Anthony.

"I don't see how you could be so close and not at least find out where she lives."

"She was like a melody. Here one minute and gone silent the next," said Anthony.

"And you're sure," said Queen Mother Rhythm, "that we're going where you were when you heard her voice?"

Before Anthony could answer, they heard the sound of singing.

"That's it," said Queen Mother Rhythm. "That's the voice!"

"Didn't I tell you?" said Anthony.

"We won't let her get away this time," said Queen Mother Rhythm.

They tried to pick up speed as they traveled forward toward the voice, but the closer they got, the shriller the wind blew, hindering their progress.

"Windy as crows all of a sudden!" declared Anthony.

"Look! We're getting closer. I can almost see her," said Queen Mother Rhythm. "This Swamp light is so strange. Now I can see her. Now I can't!"

"That's the voice. Just like I said. Like a rainbow after the storm."

Soowoosh, soowoosh, soowoosh-woosh-woosh

Then it was too windy even for crows. The dark wings of the air swooped down and took over.

"My goodness gracious. It's hard to stand!" gasped Queen Mother Rhythm.

"It's a hurricane!" shouted Anthony.

"Why now?" screamed Queen Mother Rhythm.

"Grab that tree trunk and hold on!" said Anthony.

"I'm holding! I can almost see our nightingale. We're going the distance. Hold on, sugar," Queen Mother Rhythm shouted.

"Hold on, nightingale, we're coming! Can't ten hurricanes stop me from getting to you," said Anthony.

As Queen Mother Rhythm, Anthony, and the Royal Runners dodged swaying palms and bent to the lashing wind, they heard a crash coming from the direction of where they had last heard Marigold's voice.

"Oh my God, I can't see her anymore," said Queen Mother Rhythm. "Must be the hurricane got her. Just when we found her."

"How could it be?" said Anthony as they stumbled across a felled tree spread out blocking their path. They crawled over it and kept looking, with no voice to guide them and devastation all around. They searched for as long as they could; then night pressed in on them.

Queen Mother Rhythm said sadly as they

turned back, "The girl with the nightingale song is gone."

And Anthony, River Rainbow, and Sparrow Sunrise gathered close to Queen Mother Rhythm on the long march back. Anthony's heart tore like shredded sugarcane.

CALLING THE
DREAM

JUST THE TWO of them, Anthony and Queen Mother Rhythm, early birds, prepared for practice in the Rose of Sharon sanctuary. They leafed through the hymnals and selected songs as they waited for the rest of the choir to appear.

"Do you believe the hurricane took her?" asked Anthony.

"A hurricane can be a dangerous thing," said Queen Mother Rhythm consolingly.

"I know," answered Anthony. "But something strange happened last night. A nightingale came to me in my dream and spoke, saying, 'Anthony, she's alive!'"

Queen Mother Rhythm looked at him, and it seemed like her soul filled with sadness when she saw how love made him suffer so.

"I have a plan, Queen Mother."

"What is it, son?"

"We couldn't catch the nightingale. But I know she's still alive. And there's one way to find her."

"How's that?" asked Queen Mother Rhythm.

"Let's call a Great Gospel Convention."

"A Great Gospel Convention!" Queen Mother Rhythm could already see the banner unfurled announcing the momentous occasion.

Anthony went on to explain. "We'll have voices come from miles around, and when I hear that certain pitch, I'll recognize it."

"Let's include the Silver Birds from Big Tree," said Queen Mother Rhythm.

"The Candlelights from Olive Branch," Anthony added.

"The church choirs from all over Sweet Earth," said Queen Mother Rhythm.

"We'll sit back, listen, and see if we can't find our nightingale. I've just got this feeling ⁚ . ." said Anthony.

SIGNATURE OF THE STORM

⁓

 ER HAIR tangled into elflocks, Marigold
woke up beneath the kindling stars, on her
own doorstep, as if the hurricane, when it
got finished with her, mercifully heaved her
there. "What happened?" she asked the moon
sweeping light down on her. Some of it, such
as the loss of her notebook and the sound of
thunder when it spoke in dark vowels, she recalled in minute detail. And finally standing
in the middle of the hurricane screaming. In
fact, that was the last thing she remembered.

Gardening soothed her. And so a week

later, one early morning, she listened to the language of flowers.

She inhaled deeply, and the naked lilies and lingering gardenia spoke to her through their aromas.

She contemplated their hues and they whispered the colors of buttercups and violets.

Snapdragons pressed silk into the palms of her hands.

Out of the petal shapes of daffodils, the diamond leaves of myrtle, and the round mouths of tulips, she heard "Balm. Benediction."

In the cottage as Marigold added edible violets to the green salad she tossed, Cousin Ruby was carrying on about a flyer that had come in the mail, a notice steeply lettered in muted purple and grasshopper green.

"This here is an invitation for us to appear at this Great Gospel Convention way over on the north side of the Swamp at Rose of Sharon!"

Marigold finished the salad, edged over to read over Cousin Ruby's shoulder, and exclaimed, "It says everybody's welcome."

"That's what it says all right," said Cousin Ruby. "But that's not what it means."

Carita took the paper and studied it, moving her fingers over the words as she silently mouthed them. "Mama's right," she decided. "This here's just for us. All *gifted* voices invited. Gifted. Gifted, that's us!"

"Now, Marigold," said Cousin Ruby, "I want you to get the girls ready. First you got to make them up some costumes so they'll stand out from everybody else. Then I want you to design a hairdo like none nobody's ever seen heaped on a head before—kind of like the way your head looked when that hurricane blew you in here, but pretty. I want my girls to look so sharp, their very presence will bring them some attention. Then I want you to compose a gospel song. Make it a duet—we don't want any old hymns that everybody and they mama already knows. We wanna give the people something fresh and brand-new. Make them sit up and take notice!"

"Yes ma'am," said Marigold. "Now where am I gonna find time to do all that and do the cooking, washing, and ironing? And the egg selling?"

Cousin Ruby said, "Well, you could turn your daydreaming into daydoing."

"What do you mean?" asked Marigold.

"All girls daydream," said Cousin Ruby. "I used to do some myself. What kind of dress would you wear if you could go? Design that for my daughters. What kind of song would you sing? Teach that to my daughters. How would you wear your hair?"

"Oh, I see," said Marigold.

Marigold got up and went to the battered piano. She picked at the white and black keys.

She thought she'd give the melody some chords. And so her fingers danced awhile in the lower reaches of the keyboard.

Next she added the melody on top of the chords.

"That sounds promising," said Cousin Ruby.

Marigold kept working until it was shaping up quite well.

"Let me hear you sing it," said Cousin Ruby.

"I don't think it's ready just yet," said Marigold.

"Let me hear what you've got so far."

"I need to work on finishing the chorus, got to find the right chord."

Marigold began to search among the keys as she sang the first words.

Be a rock, be an arrow
Be God's tree, be God's sparrow
And all the things
Your spirit needs to be
But most of all, be free

Ruby said, "I don't know about that 'free' part. But the rest of it sounds right. Come here, Arlita, Carita. Think you can harmonize on this thing?"

Arlita and Carita whined loudly, "Be a rock, be an arrow."

"That's not it," said Marigold. "A little softer, a little sweeter."

"Let me try by myself," huffed Carita.

And she screeched, "Be a rock, be an arrow."

Marigold's hands lifted up from the piano and covered her ears.

"Too loud! Caterwauling!" said Marigold.

"Don't be insulting my children," said Cousin Ruby. "Teach them that song. We only got two weeks."

"Not much time to turn a toad's croak into a swallow's tune. Not enough hours under the moon for that."

"What did you say?" asked Cousin Ruby.

"Nothing," said Marigold.

"Better not had," said Cousin Ruby.

"Well, while they're practicing, I can be thinking on a hairdo," said Marigold, who got up from the piano and returned to her writing table.

The twins sang, "Be a rock, be an arrow."

"That's it!" said Marigold from her writing table.

"We got it right?" exclaimed the twins.

"The hairdo," said Marigold. "I got it! It's not a hairdo at all. It's something for the hair. A crown of feathers!"

Marigold began drawing feverishly, sketching a headdress.

"Here the humble feathers from a nightingale. The iridescent plumes of a hummingbird. A peacock's pride in the curve of the line. This is it!"

"Let me see," said Cousin Ruby, reaching over her shoulder.

"Is that it?" asked the twins.

"Yes, yes, yes! My girls will draw some attention all right at the Great Gospel Convention."

"Can I go?" asked Marigold.

"What for?" asked Cousin Ruby. "You don't have no clothes. Your hair looks like a hoorah's nest, and your voice, Lord have mercy!"

"I mean," said Marigold, "maybe I could go and stand on the sidelines to make sure the girls're singing in tune."

"Let me think on it," said Cousin Ruby.

"Ma'am, every choir has a director," explained Marigold. "Every professional needs a voice coach."

"I said I'd think on it," said Cousin Ruby impatiently.

"It could be the difference between winning and losing," Marigold said, pressing her point.

Arlita and Carita chimed, "Winning and losing! Let her come. We'll have all the fun, Mama. Put her in the background somewhere, where folks can't see her."

"Now there's an idea," said Cousin Ruby. "Get to working on those costumes, Marigold."

"A dress for me would be special. It would have a rare color and wings for sleeves. Wings . . . Birds! A peacock's pride in the curve of the line," Marigold repeated to herself as she sketched the dress.

When Marigold finished the first design, it was just as she saw it in her head. "I guess that will do," she said. "When I sew the twins' dresses, there'll be plenty of material left over. I'll also make one for myself."

"Oh yes," said Cousin Ruby after Marigold had finished sketching the last dress. "This'll do just fine. Now the headpieces."

"I have to find the birds first and ask permission to use their feathers," explained Marigold.

"Permission!?" croaked Cousin Ruby. "Just go wring their necks and bring me back their colors. Today!"

And Marigold left her sketching pad and went outside, where she sat to rest for just a minute under a tree. She was so tired from working without a break that she fell asleep and dreamed of birds. She dreamed of singing birds in peacock colors, in iridescent hummingbird colors, in muted nightingale colors. In her dream she beckoned them, saying, "Pretty birds come here, let me borrow your feathers."

"What will they do to you if you return with no feathers?" asked the Nightingale.

"They'll hurt me," Marigold confided. "I do hope you'll let me borrow your feathers."

"My feathers are not so valuable," said the Nightingale. "What you need are peacock feathers."

The Peacock didn't say anything but kept his distance and started turning, displaying his fabulous plumes, spreading his regal tail of iridescent greens, purples, blues—brilliant colors with symmetrical shapes that looked like eyes when he fanned himself.

"Mr. Peacock," asked Marigold, "may I have some of your feathers?"

"I don't think so," said the Peacock. "I don't lend anybody my feathers!"

"Oh please," said Marigold. "Just a few, just a couple?"

But the Peacock would not relent.

The Nightingale went over to Marigold and whispered something in her ear.

She replied to the Nightingale, "They have to be special peacock feathers."

The Nightingale repeated, "Special peacock feathers!?"

Then regretfully added, "Around here we only got run-of-the-mill feathers. Peacock, have you seen any special peacock feathers around here? I don't know when it was the last time that I saw some special peacock feathers. Ten years ago, maybe. Once in a blue moon you'll hear tell of special peacock feathers. Right, Peacock? Oh, well, we could fly by your house and let you know if we hear of . . ."

All the while the Peacock had been hopping up and down on one foot, trying to get their attention. He finally got a word in: "Special peacock feathers—here!" He plucked a plume and handed it to Marigold. "I remember when I grew this one. There was a rainbow in the sky." He plucked some more. "There was an eclipse when this bunch appeared. You won't find these colors on any other peacock."

"Why thank you, Peacock," said Marigold.

Then the Hummingbird said, "I move so fast, you'll have to catch me, but you're welcome to take a gleaming shining piece of any part of me you can take hold of."

And Marigold had to move quickly, darting around a tree with the Hummingbird, who flitted from branch to branch. She kept missing him but finally plucked a couple of his iridescent feathers. He tired her out.

Next when she turned to the Nightingale, the Nightingale said humbly, "My feathers are not so pretty, Marigold. My strut is not so witty."

"But Nightingale," said Marigold, "the moonlight in your song is so true, I can't leave you out. Do you think you could help me with a song?" There was a melody that she associated with her mother. She didn't know why she did, but every time this melody came to her, she thought about her mother, this faceless woman. It had a plaintive air, with complex shapes that she could almost touch.

"I'll see what I can do," said the Nightingale.

"There's this one song I know," said Marigold. "I know a little bit of it. I don't know why I know it. Nobody ever taught it to me—I've just known it all my life. All I need is the rest of the words and the rest of the melody."

"My dear," said the Nightingale, "you already have them. I've just heard you describe an ailment that humans get when they've been lied to too much and shut off from their heart's song. Has anybody ever made you stop singing against your will?"

"Yes, they have," whispered Marigold.

"I knew it!" exclaimed the Nightingale. "You had an oppressed look about your left eye and your right ear. You can be cured if you're willing to take the cure."

"I'm willing," said Marigold.

"You must believe," said the Nightingale, "that you have the song within your heart. You must believe with all the belief you can muster; you must believe that you can sing it *all*, not some. And when you start to sing, you must sing from your heart and trust that the song will come."

"I don't know," said Marigold, a little hesitantly.

"Another thing, I just remembered," continued the Nightingale, encouraging her. "While you sing from your heart, a nightingale must sing from his heart to yours. You see, the music and the lyrics of our heart's song go to the darkest regions of the deepest parts of our soul. If we don't let it out enough, sometimes it can't find its way back. But when the nightingale sings the right song to your heart, a clear path is lit for the song to return."

Marigold started to sing slowly, trying hard to believe, while the Nightingale whispered in her right ear (the oppressed ear) and then later in her left ear, alternating as Marigold continued to sing.

Something kind of precious
Something kind of dear
Sparrows light on my fence every
  morning
Swallows watch me play at noon
Nightingales perch by my bedroom
  window
And whisper . . .

She stumbled through the song until she sang it clearly. She sang more words; the whole song came to her, all the way through.

Just after she thanked the Nightingale for the song, Marigold sighed happily in her sleep.

The last thing she remembered before waking up were these words from the Nightingale: "When the nightingale sings the right song to your heart, a clear path is lit for the song to return."

Marigold woke up refreshed and went to look for bird feathers. Sometimes they got hung in trees and on the bushes and in odd places on the ground. As she picked up a wild peacock's feather, she turned it thoughtfully over in her hand. And there seemed to be a path of feathers that she had never noticed before. And she picked them up, one by one. She discovered the feathers of a hummingbird in a custard apple tree. But she had a time finding any feathers of the nightingale.

She searched and searched. Because the nightingale feathers were nothing special to look at, they were harder to find. She had to look for over an hour, going deeper into the Swamp, before she found a feather lying on top of a piece of silvery metal sticking up out of the ground.

She reached for the feather. There was only one. This one would go on her headpiece alone, she decided.

When she picked up the feather, she could see that the silvery metal was part of a box. She wondered what the box was doing buried there, with just a little piece of itself sticking out, shining dully. Maybe, she thought, the hurricane had unearthed it.

Marigold dug the little box up, brushed the dirt off it, opened it, and found a pack of envelopes with a speckled green ribbon tied around them. The envelopes were not addressed and had never been postmarked.

"Odd," she said out loud. "Who would write a letter and never send it?"

She sat down with the feathers in her lap and untied the ribbon.

Four yellowed letters fell on top of the feathers.

And she opened the first one. The penmanship swirled neat, in round letters.

The first read:

Dear Letty,

I hear they call you Queen Mother Rhythm down there. Congratulations! You have the respect given so freely that I lack up here.

Letty, I mean Queen Mother Rhythm (smile), will you, would you please forgive me for breaking up the group? Guess we're all to blame, but mostly me. It's fall and our lives keep falling down just like the leaves. I know one thing, my sister, we don't have to die to go to heaven or hell. Sometimes it's right here on earth. Jimmy and I, we've had two miscarriages.

Your dear sister,
Melissa

Marigold's eyes grew big as she saw the writer was the sister of the person the letter was written to. And that person was Queen Mother Rhythm, the very one calling for the Great Gospel Convention! She sped on to the second one.

Dear Letty:

The big city's not at all as glamorous as we used to imagine it would be when we were three little girls playing grown-ups in Mama's high-heel shoes. High class sometimes means low-class morals. Remember how the old men used to make eyes at the young girls and we thought it was awful? Honey, you would be amazed at the goings-on up here. Sweet Jimmy tries so hard. We thought we had one job down, but lo and behold, another singer, the club owner's girlfriend, couldn't sing her way out of a paper sack, got the job. When Jimmy made a fuss about the contract, they hung him out of one of these high-rise windows and broke his collarbone. I wish we'd never left Sweet Earth. Sad to say, we haven't made any money to send to Sister and the girls. Seems like the harder we try, the worse it gets, like this heat. Will Sister ever forgive me?

Melissa

Marigold opened the third letter.

Dear Letty,

Or shall I say Queen Mother Rhythm? The people seem so unhappy up here. I sometimes think—if they could just hear the right music . . . On the streets, it's as though we're being harvested. The folks walk around with undertaker eyes. The walking Dead. It's as though a great hurricane dropped out of the sky and laid the city low. Devastation everywhere the snow flies.

People keep warm by living in gutted-out buildings. They make fires in oil barrels. They sleep on the streets with the dogs and no roof over their heads. My sister, Jimmy is getting so worn-out and weary. I won't mail this letter either, but I'm writing it anyway, just to ease my mind. My conscience? Now that's something else.

Your sister,
Melissa

Marigold rushed on to open the last and

fourth letter. Her eyes sped over the page. A chill pinched down her spine. She wondered how old the letters were. She trembled with excitement when she realized these letters had never been read by anybody but her, except for the woman writing them.

My dear sister,

I hope you're well. The lights here do not shine as bright as the stars over the Swamp in Sweet Earth on the darkest spring night. How I long for home and the smell of tulips and lilies in April and May. Oh, and a mess of good collard greens and some hot-water corn-bread like Mama used to make. You may not know it, girl, but you took the higher road, even though you never left Sweet Earth. Sweet Jimmy suffered so. We said many times we'd come home but were so shamed. When you leave in disgrace, it's impossible to return. Now I'm up here stranded. Sugar, Sweet Jimmy left, couldn't take it anymore. I guess it's hard to be a man when every time you stand up something stomps you back down. And it's harder to be a woman without sisters.

I'm pregnant again. Now what am I gonna do?

> *Your dear sister,*
> *Melissa*

Marigold's heart went out to the writer. She wondered what had happened to her. She put the letters back in their envelopes and retied them with the speckled green ribbon. She started to replace them in their box but tucked them in her pocket instead. Out of a deep feeling of respect, she buried the box in the dirt with one end sticking up, trying to leave the spot as the hurricane had left it and as she had found it.

She walked toward the cottage with her feathers, turning them over in her hands thoughtfully. But she looked longest at the nightingale's single plume.

SIGN OF THE RAINBOW

O<small>N THE SUN-DRENCHED</small> Sunday morning that the all-day Great Gospel Convention began, there appeared low in the sky a rainbow that stretched its crayoned arc from horizon to horizon.

The arc was a rare shimmering pane in the sky, for instead of the usual blend of four or five ribbons of color, all seven rays flamed over the Sugarcane Swamp and touched down to rest at both ends of the earth.

A red-and-orange umbrella topped the bow, merging into yellow, green, and blue, which danced over the indigo and violet.

When Queen Mother Rhythm got up off her knees from saying her morning prayers and saw the display, she exclaimed, "A blessing will surely come to us today, for I have seen the seven bridges of the Holy Spirit!"

As the people gathered and walked to church, they expressed their hopes for the nightingale.

"Where is the nightingale?"

"In hiding, it seems."

"Wonder if she'll come out for us?"

"Who knows?"

Sad looks claimed the faces, and to relieve the tension, the people turned the conversation toward the latest in the long, delicately balanced courting of Queen Mother Rhythm by Reverend Honeywell.

And the betting or "bounding" was on.

"They'd better hurry up and decide," said one member in a flowered hat. "Might as well enjoy whatever time they've got left. These here ain't no spring chickens. After all!"

"A good old-fashioned wedding would do the church good. Got to have something to look forward to! We need our little ceremonies and rituals!"

Before long they had reached the church door.

Every pew was filled. There were more people there than the church had ever held. The Candlelights from the west side of the Swamp, the Jubilees from way over on the east, the Prayer Wheel Quartet, amongst others. Marigold, dressed in a plain and simple brown dress, had never seen so many folks before in her whole life. And there was Ruby Lee all decked out and sitting up front, not paying attention to anybody except her twins. Marigold sat far away from them and let the sight of the whole panorama of people wash over her.

Reverend Honeywell was in top form as he preached the morning service about love. Although Marigold sat way in the back in the last pew, she could hear every syllable he spoke, his voice was so articulate. She was comfortable there where she would not be easily observed. She listened with open ears to his words about love. Love to her was synonymous with Anthony. She couldn't get her eyes full enough of him.

And Anthony was sitting in the front of the church, near the choir, where he could direct the Voices of Paradise. He was just as handsome as she remembered him. This day he looked even more mature. His face had a sculptured seriousness about it, giving an interesting effect to his inquiring eyes, his high cheekbones, his mangrove skin.

"I once again proclaim our theme for this Great Gospel Convention," said Reverend Honeywell as he waded into his sermon. "The theme, folks, is Love. Today, Church, visiting choirs, we come together to give thanks for the abundance of love surviving in our midst."

"Amen," said the congregation, and Marigold thought about Anthony and the nightingale feather in her purse, the feather she would slip into her headdress just before the sing-off began. For some reason, every time she thought about the feather, she thought of Anthony.

"Now, some of us," said Reverend Honeywell, "do get a little confused from time to time. We get Love and Lust all mixed up."

"Well," said Queen Mother Rhythm, over

in the Amen Corner, giving that echoing ritual so familiar in the call-and-response part of the sermon.

Ruby was thinking, I know what he's talking about. Love and Lust. Hah! Look where it's got me!

"Whereas," continued Reverend Honeywell, "the Bible mentions love thirty-one times, it mentions lust only three times."

"Come on out with it then," said Queen Mother Rhythm.

Marigold couldn't help but whisper to one of the latecomers sitting next to her, "Is that the Minister of Music over there?"

"Sure is. Anthony's his name. Been loving music since he was a little baby. I was there the day he crawled over and pushed down the pedals on the piano Letty was playing so he could hear the difference in the sound. Couldn't talk or walk, but he knew he wanted to make music. Been making it ever since. The youngest Minister of Music in the country, I bound you."

"Oh" was all Marigold could say. His passion for music matched hers. "And is that Queen Mother Rhythm over there in the

Amen Corner?" She was thinking about the letters she held addressed to Queen Mother.

"None but," said the member, pointing to Queen Mother Rhythm fanning herself with the church fan. The church member looked at Marigold, noticed her staring, and said, "Everybody knows Reverend Honeywell's in love with her."

"He is?" said Marigold, who listened on to Reverend Honeywell with renewed interest. She thought about that song she had written, "Something Kind of Precious." Like some word on the tip of your tongue, the song waited on the tip of her mind.

"Imagine, if you will," she heard Reverend Honeywell saying, "that Lust and Love had a battle. It was a battle for life. Lust said, 'I am the baddest, *for whosoever even looketh on a woman to lust after her hath committed adultery with her already in his heart.'"

"So the Bible says," agreed Queen Mother Rhythm, rocking in her corner.

"Love said, 'I don't mean to brag, Mr. Lust, but my love is so great that I love my enemies, bless them that curse me, do good to them that despitefully use me.'"

"Preach it!" said the congregation.

Marigold could see the same longing in Anthony's face that she saw mirrored in Reverend Honeywell's. He's still in love with that other girl, Marigold thought.

Now her attention went back to Reverend Honeywell. "'Oh,' said Mr. Lust, 'you're talking about the flesh now. *I make not provisions for the flesh to fulfill the lusts thereof.* Romans, thirteenth chapter and the fourteenth verse.'"

"Make it plain," sang the congregation.

Reverend Honeywell preached on. "Love said, 'You a backward liar, Mr. Lust.' Don't you know," said Reverend Honeywell, "sometimes the Devil can quote the Bible better than the saints. Mr. Love said, 'You got the context wrong, Mr. Lust. The thirteenth verse just before that says, *Let us walk honestly, as in the day; not in rioting and drunkenness, not in chambering and wantonness, not in strife and envying. But put ye on the Lord Jesus Christ and make not provision for the flesh, to fulfill the lusts thereof.*'"

"Amen and amen!" said the congregation. The melancholy Anthony was quiet, as if searching for a message in the sermon that might lead to his love.

Reverend Honeywell continued, "Lust said, 'And I don't want to know about your God. I come from another kingdom. I'm so bad, your Bible put out a warning against me, talking about *Abstain from fleshly lusts, which war against the soul.*'"

"Satan, the Lord rebuke you," chanted Queen Mother Rhythm, waving her handkerchief.

Reverend Honeywell preached, "You know what Love did? Do you know what he did? He gave Mr. Lust one of them looks. You all know the kind of look I'm talking about. You see Love, old Love was getting ready for the knockout punch, because he knew old Lust didn't have anything left. Love leaned back and said, '*He that loveth not, knoweth not God, for God is love.* Mr. Lust, you're all about negativity, you're all about fear.' Mr. Love said, '*There is no fear in love; but perfect love casteth out fear.*'"

And Marigold saw a fleeting smile claim Anthony's face. Hope all in it.

"But not for me," whispered Marigold. She thought about the letters and the lost love between Queen Mother Rhythm, her two sisters, and that man Sweet Jimmy. She wondered about the sisterly love that Melissa the letter writer missed.

"With those words," continued the minister, "*There is no fear in love; but perfect love casteth out fear,* Love scored a powerful blow."

And Reverend Honeywell took on the stance of a boxer as he continued to preach and punch his way through the sermon so dramatically that Marigold thought he would make an excellent actor. "Lust fell out like a rock," said Reverend Honeywell with his arms stretched out in defeat, "lay stretched out on the canvas. He was down for the count and Love commenced to delivering more and more Love ammunition.

"He said, '*Owe no man anything, but to love one another.*' Let me tell you something else he said: '*Love is the fulfilling of the law.*' Love went on, said: '*A new commandment I give unto you, that you love one another,* John, the thirteenth chapter and the thirty-fourth verse. *For God so loved the world, that he gave his only* begotten *Son, that whosoever believeth in him should not perish, but have everlasting life.* John, third chapter, sixteenth verse.'"

"Speak the truth!" exclaimed Queen Mother Rhythm, who was now so caught up in the sermon, she was rocking back and forth.

And Marigold's and Anthony's eyes stayed glued on the preacher, both listening for answers.

Reverend Honeywell preached on, wrapped up in the sermon. "And while Mr. Lust was lying there like the Devil's own soldier without his shield, like a hypocrite without a hip to prop his hands on, Love went on and added, '*Set me as a seal upon thine heart, as a seal upon thine arm: for love is strong as death; jealousy is cruel as the grave,* Song of Solomon, eighth chapter, sixth verse.

"'I tell you this,' said Love, '*Many waters can not quench love, neither can the floods drown it.*'"

And neither can a hurricane, thought Melissa, remembering the love letters from one sister to the other.

And Ruby Lee felt a longing for something so lovely, so sweet, as sweet as the love she had for her sisters when they were little girls—outside swinging in their swings, holding the ropes tight as they flew to one another, on the porch braiding each other's hair, in the living room wearing Mama's high-heel shoes, behind the church trying to sing like the famous blues singers.

And Marigold was thinking that if love endures hurricanes and all that, then maybe she'd always love Anthony.

At the same time she was contemplating this, a smile as broad as a sunrise claimed Anthony's face.

"I love them that love me; and those that seek me early shall find me," said Reverend Honeywell, whose rhythm and pacing told Anthony the sermon was winding down. And Anthony sat at the organ and started playing softly, accompanying Reverend Honeywell.

"After he was sure Mr. Lust had been thoroughly defeated, knocked cold, dusted, Love turned to us to instruct us how to live this present life."

All eyes were now on Queen Mother

Rhythm as Reverend Honeywell turned to preaching directly at her.

"As I end my sermon this Love Sunday, I'm going to leave you with something from the Song of Solomon, second chapter, tenth to the twelfth verses," said Reverend Honeywell. *"Rise up, my love, and come away. For, lo! the winter is past, the rain is over and gone; the flowers appear on the earth; and the time of the singing of birds is come. . . ."*

And for the second time Marigold heard Anthony's singing voice, when he led the song, "Love."

The Voices of Paradise came in on the chorus, chanting "Love lives in me, God's love."

Reverend Honeywell recited, his speaking voice riding over the song, *"And Jacob served seven years for Rachel; and they seemed to him but a few days, for the love he had."*

Those words seemed to pull Queen Mother Rhythm right out of her chair. After all these years, Letty realized, Reverend Honeywell is right about the text he preached today. And she walked to the podium and joined Reverend Honeywell, repeating the words, "And they say *Jacob served seven years for Rachel; and they seemed but a few days, for the love.*" Then the two of them stood up there and sang like two lovebirds:

> *In love there is no fear*
> *Makes a century seem like a year*
> *When my years seem like a few days*
> *Love speaks to me in timeless ways*
> *Love lives in me*
> *God's love*

Marigold turned to the member who had pointed out Anthony and Queen Mother Rhythm earlier to her and said, "I guess Queen Mother Rhythm and Reverend Honeywell will get married after all."

"That's right, sugar," agreed her neighbor as they both stood up from the pew to recite the benediction, signaling the end of the morning service.

MUSIC AND
MEMORY

I N HER POCKET not only did Marigold carry
the feather from the nightingale, but she also
carried the packet of letters that she knew belonged to Queen Mother Rhythm.

She had decided that if Queen Mother
Rhythm spoke to her today, she would take
the opportunity to hand over the letters from
her sister, Melissa. She could barely wait for
the gospel contest to begin, but first they all
had to rehearse and get into their costumes.

While they were setting up for the first
group to come on, Marigold kept trying to
get a glimpse of Anthony. He seemed to be in

charge of everything, although everyone knew Queen Mother Rhythm was the name that was used to call the gospel convention together.

"Let's check out the sound system," he said to River Rainbow and Sparrow Sunrise, who were dressed in overalls, carrying golden cables of speaker wire.

"Testing, one, two, three," he said into first one microphone, then the next. The third one needed work.

"Hey, must be a wire loose here." And he followed the wire from the mike to the speakers and hooked up a loose plug.

"Testing, one, two, three," he spoke again into the third microphone, and this time his ginger voice was wonderfully clear.

She was staring at him so hard that he could feel it, but when he turned toward her direction, she turned her back and looked off somewhere else.

Still she had to look again. Couldn't keep her eyes off him. He was a feast for her hungry glance. And she stuffed herself on the luscious sight of him.

He worked with his sleeves rolled up, his tie loosened, his jacket parked on the back of the piano bench.

After he finished checking out the sound system to his satisfaction, he rearranged the chairs in the choir stand so that the singers, no matter the number, could stand in a semicircle. Almost any seat in the place would be a good seat, Marigold realized.

It was while she was looking at him that the first verse of that lost song, the song she had written, came back to her. She flushed with excitement. Maybe all she had to do was steal a few glances at him and that song lingering on the tip of her mind would come flying back to her.

"Something Kind of Precious" started spinning in her head. And she wished she had brought paper with her. A notebook, but she had not written any lyrics to that song since she had lost the notebook. It was painful to her to remember all the lost words. All the lost work.

But she needed a pen and paper right away.

There were flyers all around—on the pews, on the walls—announcing the Great Gospel Convention.

"I'm sure they won't mind my borrowing a couple of pages," she said.

"What do you think you're doing?" Cousin Ruby asked, when she and the twins joined her.

Oh shoot! thought Marigold. Now I'll never get to that song.

"I was just picking up some of these as souvenirs. I'm sure you'll want them as mementos when the twins win the sing-off."

The minute she could get out of sight of Cousin Ruby and the twins, she walked around staying out of the way, observing, listening, appreciating the different-colored gospel robes the singers wore and the long, formal gowns of the solo singers, some with stars, beads, spangles.

Songs flew around her everywhere, as different groups practiced for the big event.

At last she saw the woman who had pointed out Queen Mother Rhythm to her and asked, "Do you happen to have a pen or pencil I might borrow?"

"Let me see," said the young woman. And she rummaged around in her purse, "I thought . . ." Seeing the wistful look on Marigold's face, she turned the purse upside down, spilling out lipstick, powder, perfume, handkerchief, flyer, a little Bible, and at last a pen. "Well, guess you're in luck, my little friend," said the young woman.

And Marigold accepted the pen. "I'll give it back to you later."

"Oh, that's all right. I don't need it."

Outside, Marigold found a little knoll under a tree and sat herself down on the grass.

At the top of the back of the flyer, she wrote, "Something Kind of Precious."

And then she kept in front of her mind how Anthony looked when he was fixing the microphones and the words started coming back to her.

Something kind of precious
Something kind of dear
Sparrows light on my fence every morning
Swallows watch me play at noon

She looked up, and lo and behold, here came Cousin Ruby and the twins. "Yoo hoo,

Marigold!" said Cousin Ruby, on her best public behavior because people were milling around. The way she said Marigold's name was too sweet, and Marigold cringed as she put away the song and the pen.

When they got to where she sat, Cousin Ruby said, "It's time to get dressed. Everybody else is just about ready, but I haven't seen any outfits that even come close to what my dear little twins will be wearing."

"Now that's the truth," said Marigold.

"Come on."

And so Marigold got up and they got their bags packed with the newly-sewn dresses, found the bathroom just about free now, and put on their clothes. Marigold put the headdresses on Arlita and Carita, and then she put her own on her head, first slipping the nightingale feather in the band among the peacock and hummingbird feathers.

"Yours looks a little different," said Cousin Ruby, staring at Marigold.

"Each one is a little different since they're handmade. That's why they're showstoppers."

At the answer, showstoppers, Cousin

Ruby cooed happily, "The best outfits at this convention. I'm glad I thought this up."

"Thought this up?" said Marigold, wondering how Cousin Ruby could take credit for her creation.

"Well, I was the one who told you to design the dresses," said Cousin Ruby with pride.

"That's right," said Marigold.

Just then the organ began playing, as a signal that the convention was about to begin, rehearsal time was over, and everyone had to take their places.

As packed as the church was in the morning, now it was packed with the same crowd of folks, in vibrant, colored robes. A rainbow of sight.

Reverend Honeywell said his blessing over the entire affair.

Then the reverend sat down next to Queen Mother Rhythm in her reviewing chair. And on the other side of her sat Anthony, meticulously dressed. In a subtly patterned black-on-blue suit of the newest style. But mostly he glowed with color from a rainbow within, that no suit could even hope to match.

WHERE IS
THE ANGEL?

Across the back of the church choir stand hung the banner proclaiming, "THE GREAT GOSPEL CONVENTION: THE THEME IS LOVE." And the breeze through the open window fluttered the large golden words on the blue cloth until everyone's eyes had to settle on the announcement from time to time. And Anthony stood back and surveyed the work he had done on the choir stand. He said to Queen Mother Rhythm, "Queen Mother, I liked that group from Pine Tree and the Sounds of Wonder were wonders. But some of these groups, have you ever heard so much howling and hooting enough to hurt your nerves?"

"Never," Queen Mother Rhythm agreed. "I hope this works, Anthony. If we find our nightingale, it's worth all this aggravation."

They were on to group twenty, and the night was growing long.

Then Anthony rose, went to the microphone, and announced the next group.

"Coming to you all the way from the other side of the Swamp," said Anthony, "please welcome the Trumpeteers!"

The Trumpeteers rolled the drums and bounced tambourines off their hips, and the women looked different from the other women's groups, for they were dressed not in robes but in street clothes, dresses showing thighs, slits, low-cut bosoms exposing the tops of breasts. But worst of all, they jazzed up "Steal Away" and popped their fingers.

"Steal away, steal away, steal away to Jesus." Before they could begin the second verse, Reverend Honeywell said, "Anthony, Anthony, sound the gong. Imagine popping their fingers on a spiritual song! 'Do Jesus.' 'Steal on away from here.' That ain't it. Ain't no nightingale hanging 'round this motley, skip-dipping, snake-hipping crew!"

Anthony hurried to the microphone after letting the choir finish their first of what was to have been three numbers and said, "We've got a time problem, folks. We're moving on to the next group."

Next came the Caroleers singing "Didn't My Lord Deliver Daniel?"

They sang off key, "He delivered Daniel from the lion's den, Jonah from the belly of the whale, and the Hebrew children from the fiery furnace, and why not every man?"

Reverend Honeywell and Queen Mother Rhythm looked at each other, and already Anthony was up out of his seat when they began the chorus, "Didn't my Lord deliver Daniel?"

Reverend Honeywell said, "I don't know about Daniel. But He sure can deliver me. That ain't it. Hand clapping's off, not to mention the beat. The Devil come by here early and got in their feet!"

"Next we have the Twins of Harmony," Anthony announced.

"Ain't those the children whose mama

been worrying us half to death with letters about how great they are? I don't know. Anthony already . . ." said Queen Mother Rhythm, her voice drifting off.

She was so tired, she yawned and her head began to hang a little.

Uh-oh, thought Anthony, Queen Mother's flagging, getting tired; it's break time.

From her place behind the curtain, Marigold looked longingly at Anthony. And as Anthony stepped to the side as the people left the choir stand, Marigold could have almost reached out and touched him.

Where is our nightingale? Anthony wondered. Did she make it through the storm? We've been through fifty-eleven voices, and I still haven't heard her sweet song. If I should even hear her whisper, I'd know it.

Marigold, watching him intently from behind the curtain, heard him say under his breath, "Where is that angel whose voice I heard?"

He's still pining after that old other girl. Shoot! thought Marigold, and she came from behind the curtain and went and sat sulking in a side pew out of sight of everyone.

She overheard two of the Voices of Paradise gossiping during the break.

"Doesn't look too good," said Betty Jean. "Think we'll ever find a replacement for Queen Mother Rhythm?"

"Well," said Annie Mae, "the voice's got to be an original."

"Uh-huh," agreed Betty Jean, "got to have a special coloring to the timbre."

"Like Queen Mother's," said Annie Mae.

Betty Jean said, "To get that you got to've had heartbreak, like Queen Mother Rhythm. But she did steal her own sister's husband, and the younger sister turned around and stole him from them both. Then they all cursed each other. Umph. Cursing each other out! Ever heard of good Baptists doing all such as that?"

"Now tell the truth," said Annie Mae. "Can't rightly call it cursing each other out. Not four-letter-word cursing."

There was a loud clatter of a drum spangle falling, and Marigold missed Betty Jean's next sentence: "And then her dying sister's baby disappearing like that."

She did hear Annie Mae's response

though. "I just wonder when you're gonna leave other people's affairs alone. When are you gonna learn to stay out of Brother Biscuit and Sister Cornbread's business?"

"I don't see you covering your ears," said Betty Jean.

"I think she's suffered enough," said Annie Mae.

"I reckon the Lord made her suffer just so He could hear her call His name! I would if I was God."

"Don't be so mean," said Annie Mae.

"Can't nobody holler His name like Queen Mother Rhythm, the original Nightingale. *LORD!*" sang Betty Jean, mimicking Queen Mother's gospel cry.

Marigold smiled in spite of herself. The women's colorful words had put her in good humor. She looked at the paper and started the second verse of the song.

After she finished the second verse, Marigold thought she heard one of the twins calling her name, but she didn't get up to see; she wanted to finish the song while it was still coming. What was that last verse? It stubbornly stayed tucked in her mind. And then she remembered what had happened in the Swamp when she had finished the last line—the hurricane had come. That's it, she remembered. She remembered the singing of the wind. And the way the song had flowed. And the dream with the birds! "When the nightingale sings the right song from his heart to yours, a clear path is lit for the song to return." She finished it.

Now both twins were calling her name. With a relieved sigh she tucked the paper in her pocket and went to where they stood.

"We got to get up near the choir stand, since we're next on the program," said Carita.

"All right. Let's go," said Arlita.

Cousin Ruby, who was already back there, said, "Now you stay way behind the curtain, Marigold. Don't want you appearing and scaring the folk."

"What?" asked Marigold.

"Whisper," said Carita. "That's enough out of you, Marigold."

Under her breath, Marigold said, "My dream. I haven't forgotten what the Nightingale sang. He told me I was something kind of precious. First chance I get I'll test it."

"Mama," said Arlita, "it's getting smothering hot up in here. Can't we go outside for a little fresh air?"

"I see you eyeing the boys," Cousin Ruby said to Arlita. "Don't be trying to be fast around here, I say. Good-for-nothing boys'll take something precious and leave you holding the bag, the belly, and the baby."

"Umph," said Carita, who joined Arlita in eyeing Anthony.

Marigold thought, Now I see what jealousy feels like. Barbed wire to the soul! Sure wish they'd stop looking at *him*.

Carita said, "Oh, Mama! We just want to show off our new clothes and new hairdos."

"All right then," said Cousin Ruby. "You're only young once. But don't go too far. When they reconvene this convention, y'all have to sing first."

One of the other singers backstage who overheard the conversation between the twins and their mother commented, "Who she think she fooling? If those two can sing, chickens can fly."

River Rainbow and Sparrow Sunrise, who had been helping Anthony, asked, "What's the order of the program, Anthony?"

"The Twins of Harmony are on next, but I do think the people are tired of all these awful voices. We may have to pause and let them hear Queen Mother Rhythm before we go on further."

As if on cue, an irate woman in the audience called out as the people filed back in, "I didn't come clean 'cross Alligator Alley and Possum Pasture to hear all this ungodly singing." And then she fainted.

"Somebody just passed out in the audience," said Anthony.

"Go rouse Queen Mother Rhythm," said River Rainbow to Sparrow Sunrise.

"No, Lord, not me. Face the wrath of her mouth? She's a mighty sweet woman, but I don't think she was counting on singing at this convention. Only judging."

"All right, I'll do it," said Anthony.

And he crossed the choir stand to where Queen Mother Rhythm was resting behind a partition.

"Queen Mother Rhythm!" Anthony whispered.

But Queen Mother Rhythm breathed

deeply, sleeping so soundly that she didn't hear him at first. Cousin Ruby, hunkered down behind the partition, was trying to get the edge on what was going on.

"Pssst," she said to Anthony. "Course I could try to take over for her."

Anthony, usually extremely polite, had just about had it. His nerves had been worn to a frazzle by some of the untalented voices. He didn't even hear the sound of rain beating hard against the window when Cousin Ruby spoke to him, and so he responded without much thought.

"Woman," he said, "I can look at you and tell you can't sing straight. There's something fairly crooked about your spirit. Loose here, Satan. Straighten up now. God uses intelligent people. Why, those two daughters of yours look like they don't have sense enough to come in out of the rain!"

Thunder rumbled from far off, then nearer, and the rain gathered strength as it pelted against the church roof.

"Rain!?" said Cousin Ruby. "Carita! Arlita!" she called as she started running to fetch them.

Carita and Arlita appeared before she could get their names out good, but they were all drenched. Their headpieces were twisted and ruined, and their dresses dripping wet.

Anthony gently shook Queen Mother Rhythm. "Queen Mother Rhythm?"

She stirred herself awake, fanning.

"It's so hot, Anthony, I declare. Feels like a storm brewing. Gets this hot, nothing left for God to do but send some rain."

"He did," said Anthony. "The next act got drenched, and they need to dry out. Could you fill in for us, Queen Mother Rhythm?"

"Me?" said Queen Mother Rhythm. "That's not why we convened this convention. How're we gonna find the new nightingale when I'm up there singing?"

Just then Reverend Honeywell showed up as a reinforcement. He said, "Please sing for us."

"Well, if you say so."

A Nightingale
Takes to
the Sky

Queen Mother Rhythm, Reverend Honeywell, and Anthony returned to the reviewing chairs. After a pause when he was certain that the entire audience was reseated, Anthony stepped up to the microphone.

"Well," Anthony cheerfully informed the congregation, "looks like we're gonna have to make a little addition to the program. Indeed. Looks like a change is very much called for. Our own Queen Mother Rhythm will come forth and render us a selection."

As the Queen made her way to the podium, the audience broke out into a thunderous applause. Here was exactly what the program needed. But before she began to sing, Queen Mother Rhythm recalled, "For years I wanted to be Queen Mother Rhythm. Well, now I'm getting ready to retire as lead singer of the choir. We've called this Great Gospel Convention together so that we might discover a new nightingale. My spirit tells me that she's here somewhere in this crowd of singers tonight.

"It's been a long day and we've heard groups from all over Sweet Earth.

"And now, folks, night has fallen. Just look at the moon peeping yonder through the window. Full and silver. Shining the way it shined many moons ago when I first got called the original Nightingale."

And then a great hush seemed to fall over the hall as Queen Mother Rhythm started her song, "The Heavenly Choir."

> *I'm getting ready to go to the heavenly*
> *   choir*
> *Got my ticket in my hand*
> *Got my suitcase packed for a faraway*
> *   land*

I'm getting ready to join the heavenly choir

A musical interlude followed, spirited, with much clapping as the choir came in on the chorus, singing "Yes we will" when Queen Mother Rhythm sang the question "Will you be ready?"

She sang the song fully, much the way she used to sing when she first led the choir, giving the listeners the full measure of her bountiful voice.

A sigh of satisfaction sifted through the crowd when Queen Mother Rhythm finished and returned to her chair. Everybody's spirit was eased a little bit.

Anthony went to the microphone and asked, "Is everybody happy?!"

"Yes!" rang out the enthusiastic crowd.

"All right then," said Anthony. "Guess we're ready now to bring on the next group. Trying to find us a new nightingale. Folks, I present to you the Twins of Harmony."

The pianist struck up a ta-ta-ta-da chord as Arlita and Carita, all dried off now but a little rumpled, approached the microphone, opened their mouths, and sang, "When your life is dim, and everything looks so grim, you can't get a prayer through to God."

"Just look what the storm blew in," cried Betty Jean to Annie Mae. "Looking like that, trying to sing for God. Singing harmony crooked as two crows."

People sagged in their seats. Querulous voices hooted from the outraged mouths. Many wondered if a nightingale would ever rise up among them and take wing.

Queen Mother Rhythm didn't say a word. She got up from her reviewing chair and started to exit.

The whole place teetered on the edge of pandemonium.

Cousin Ruby whispered to Marigold desperately, "Pssst. Help them out!"

And Marigold took up the song from where she stood behind the curtain.

> *And you just can't see the sun*
> *Be a rock, be an arrow*
> *Be a tree, be a sparrow*
> *And all the things*

Your spirit wants to be
But most of all, be free

The entire church settled into quietness and seemed to sway under a sanctified spell.

Queen Mother Rhythm stopped in her tracks. She couldn't breathe as Marigold continued.

You came into this world
All on your own
But there are people just like you
Just meet them and you will see
You'll never be alone

Be a rock, be an arrow
Be a tree, be a sparrow
And all the things
Your spirit wants to be
But most of all, be free

And she held on to that last note as though it was life itself. And the fainting woman who had passed out earlier stood up revived and waved her handkerchief. People who had looked tired just a few minutes before found new life and sat up taller in their pews. Sleeping babies woke up and started cooing. Older people laid down their canes and limped up out of their wheelchairs.

And Anthony said, "That voice!"

"Sing it again!" someone in the audience chanted in a raspy shout.

And Marigold did. The people's spirits seemed to rise as one with the song until they were all changed into higher beings with angel wings.

Queen Mother Rhythm finally caught her breath and said, "Where's that voice coming from?"

Anthony found himself moving behind the curtain, where he discovered Marigold dressed in her splendid dress, her regal headpiece. He took her hands and looked deeply into her eyes.

"Why you're gorgeous—your skin mahogany with a red-flower voice to match. I've waited so long!"

And Queen Mother Rhythm was chanting, "That's the song! That's the voice! So old. So young."

And Anthony was saying, "So pure. So fine. Here is the angel I heard."

He took her hand and led her to front center of the choir stand. All eyes were on her now.

Marigold couldn't believe her ears. "And all the time it was me you were thinking about?" When he touched her, a current lifted her spirit high as a palm tree. There were singing birds in her head. And a red flower opened and brushed against each of her cheeks.

Cousin Ruby, cowering by the side of the choir stand, exclaimed, "That heifer done stole the song, stole the show, and stole the title!" Then she said to Marigold, "Who told you you could sing?"

"A little bird," said Marigold.

"Who is she to you?" asked Queen Mother Rhythm.

"She ain't nobody," said Cousin Ruby. "A chance child. Her own mama abandoned her. Just up and left the little wretch. So I took her in."

Queen Mother Rhythm leaned forward and recognized her own sister, whom she had not seen for years.

"Ruby Lee? It *is* you. I thought so! Baby

stealer! Woman, you lie. Our own sister, Melissa, died giving her birth. Where were you the day she was born? How did you up and steal the child? She was our own sister, knowing she was dying, bringing her child to me. This is our blood, my niece. I'd know our sister's gospel voice anywhere. I can hear it all in her daughter's breath. You should know it too!"

"No she's not," insisted Cousin Ruby. "I found her in the bushes. Rescued her from the stickers and the weeds."

"What's your name, sugar?" Queen Mother Rhythm asked Marigold.

"Marigold."

"I gave the baby to a Swamp Woman. She was standing in a bed of marigolds," said Queen Mother Rhythm. "Ruby Lee, you snatched her and give her that name."

Queen Mother Rhythm walked toward Cousin Ruby and drew her out near the center of the choir stand. "Don't be trying to hide. Come on, out with it then. Yes. It's you, Ruby Lee!"

Finally Ruby Lee said in a contrite tone, finally seeing what she'd done, aware that there was something in Marigold's voice that she had envied, that she had hated, "Well, we, my daughters and I, we were just trying to be good Samaritans. That's right. Good Samaritans. We gave her a home. See how fine she's dressed. We treated her just like one of the family. We didn't know she was kin. This old Swamp Woman left her on my doorstep. Said the baby belonged to me because she looked like me. I don't know what she was talking about. I never saw her or that baby before in my life. She kept muttering something about marigolds . . ."

Then Carita piped up, "Them's our clothes. She's just the maid. She ain't nohow fit to sing at conventions and other high places like us. Mama said we come from a singing family.

"That's our headpiece," said Arlita. "She was just modeling. Even if she did make it with her own hands."

Queen Mother Rhythm folded her arms across her chest and said, "I guess that's your song, too, she's singing."

"As a matter of fact," said Carita, "it is. Mama made her make it up just for us."

"At last we've found our nightingale," said Anthony, who couldn't take his eyes off Marigold.

An old anger rose up in Queen Mother Rhythm as she spoke to Ruby. She said, "How could you treat this child this way, Ruby Lee?"

Ruby Lee kept shaking her head. "I didn't know she was flesh and blood. I didn't know."

"You didn't know?" said Queen Mother Rhythm. "Whether someone is kin or not shouldn't make any difference to how you treat that person. The Bible says *Be not forgetful to entertain strangers: for thereby some have entertained angels unawares.* Did that cup of bitterness that man left you make you blind to compassion? This child ain't had nothing to do with that old feud."

"That's the truth," said Annie Mae on the sidelines listening. "That feud's so old it's mildewed. Cursing each other like that at a gospel convention. *Sweet* Jimmy left a *bitter* taste. All these wasted years! Jealousy sure is cruel, cruel to the grave!"

Reverend Honeywell lowered his head and

prayed, arms stretched toward heaven, "Come into our midst, oh Lord!"

Annie Mae said, "God ain't thinking about coming down here making these daughters sing."

"Now that's the truth," said Queen Mother Rhythm. "But this nightingale can sing sweet enough for all of us."

Then, turning to Cousin Ruby, she said, "Look at Marigold, won't you? Looking just like your husband, her father, and our sister, Melissa."

Marigold pulled her eyes away from Anthony's long enough to say, "Father? I never knew my father."

"We sure did!" said Queen Mother Rhythm and Cousin Ruby.

"Oh, I just remembered something," said Marigold. And she reached in her pocket and got out the batch of letters. "I found these buried in the Swamp. I think they belong to you."

Queen Mother Rhythm looked at the speckled green ribbon and paled. "Swamp Woman must have hidden them." As she untied the packet, her hands trembled. When she opened the first letter her eyes blurred. "Oh my dear lost sister and your poor lost mama. Honey, these letters were written by your mother's hand," she said.

Pulling herself together Queen Mother Rhythm said, "New nightingale, we're glad you're here."

"My stepdaughter, my daughter," Cousin Ruby said hesitating, her mind whirling. "I've done wrong by you, Marigold." These were the hardest words she ever spoke. "Forgive me. I forgive Letty. I forgive Melissa. And that crooked Jimmy." She whispered in a broken voice, "Marigold, can you ever forgive me?"

"Oh, sister. Oh, sister, can you forgive us?" chimed the twins following their mother's lead.

Anthony said, "What do you think, Marigold?"

"I know one thing," said Marigold in a quiet voice. "I don't believe God's got anything to do with these old curses. I've listened to everybody speak and looks like I took the brunt of this old feud. Hurt is hurt, even if the person doing it doesn't know she's hurting her own kin.

"But," she added, taking a deep breath, "I suspect when folks curse each other, the only one who can get rid of it is the one who called it."

"It's over," said Queen Mother Rhythm.

"Forgotten," agreed Cousin Ruby.

"Now, Marigold," said Anthony, proud of the way she resolved the situation, "these sisters of yours may not sing like they're kin to you, but every bird in the sky's not a nightingale. Just like every member of the choir's not a Queen Mother Rhythm. Where would a song be without the background singers? These here twins are the Nightingale Background Singers. I think I might could mold them into shape."

"Oh, please do!" said Carita and Arlita.

"Harmony," said Reverend Honeywell. "That's what puts the honey in life. It takes more than one to harmonize. Queen Mother Rhythm, will you marry me?"

"Why, Reverend," said Queen Mother Rhythm, "I thought you'd never ask. My answer is Yes."

"Nightingale, nightingale, can you sing for us now?"

And Marigold began "Something Kind of Precious."

> *Something kind of precious*
> *Something kind of dear*

"Let's hear the harmony," said Anthony.

And the twins sang in harmony because they were a family now.

> *Something kind of precious*
> *Something kind of dear*

And Marigold stretched out on the song.

> *Sparrows light on my fence every morning*
> *Swallows watch me play at noon*
> *Nightingales perch by my bedroom*
>   *window*
> *And whisper me this evening tune*
> *Something kind of precious*
> *Something kind of dear*
>
> *Something kind of precious*
> *Something kind of dear*
>
> *Now they might try to take your song*
> *Try it if they dare*

But if your song reach out and grab them
Don't say we didn't tell them to beware
  'cause

Sparrows light on your fence every
  morning
Swallows watch you play at noon
Nightingales perch by your bedroom
  window
And whisper you this evening tune
Something kind of precious
Something kind of dear

Something kind of precious
Something kind of dear

Queen Mother Rhythm announced, "The choice has been made and the new nightingale has arrived. She took a long time to get here, but she wasn't a second too late. It gives me great delight to pass the title on to my niece, Marigold. The journeys we take in life never unfold like we would have them unfold. Marigold, daughter, listen to the song your heart is singing now, not the one it sang yesterday and not the one it wants to sing tomorrow. And don't be shocked when the tune changes, because it's just our souls trying to tell us that it's time to move on in a different way."

And Anthony took Marigold's hand and led her to her place in the choir where the Nightingale traditionally stood. As he sat down at the piano to direct the song, Marigold took the lead.

And so she found her family and her place. And her aunts who were enemies became friends. And her cousins who were bickerers became harmonizers. And her boy became her man. And her song remained her own.

JOYCE CAROL THOMAS
was born in Oklahoma and currently lives near Knoxville, Tennessee, where she is a professor of English at the University of Tennessee, teaching creative writing. Ms. Thomas won the National Book Award for her first novel, *Marked by Fire*. She is also a playwright and a poet.